Harvest Moon

by

Summer Lee
The Stargazers Trilogy #2

Harvest Moon
Published by Summer Lee
Copyright © 2016 by Summer Lee

Dedication
To Manuel.

CONTENTS

HARVEST MOON

CHAPTER ONE

For the third straight day a relentless rain fell. It felt eerie and supernatural.

Christians knew that God wouldn't flood the earth again. He made a promise to Noah and they believed He would keep His word. Non-Christians weren't so confident.

Bitter winds succeeded in making the rain feel like ice shards were pelting those unfortunate enough to be caught in the storm. Most people in the area stayed indoors. The only ones who dared to venture out were the ones who absolutely had to. So, the streets were mostly vacant. Police officers and other emergency workers were the only people seen with any regularity.

There was one odd exception. The graves of Sybil and Eric Tania and Isabella had a visitor.

The cemetery was practically flooded, which made it almost impossible for those who wished to pay their respects to the dead. The caretakers had hired more people to keep up with the maintenance and care of each plot. Of course, the more expensive the grave, better and more frequent care was administered.

Solomon had bought a family plot and had his three friends caskets moved there together. The graves of Sybil and Eric Tania and Isabella sat side by side as a grim reminder to anyone knowledgeable of the events that had transpired during the Blood Moons several months ago. Some of the dirt had washed away and Eric's headstone was tilted to one side. The other two headstones were just as straight as the day they had been placed.

The lone figure stood reflecting on the three plots. No movement. No tears. Just a whispered prayer for mercy. It was the first time anyone had visited the graves. he made it a point to visit at least once a month.

A year had passed since Isabella's and Eric's headstones had been placed. One whole year had gone by since the world had nearly ended. There were a few who remembered the events that had transpired nearly bringing about Armageddon. The rest of the world forgot about it within days, and they went on living as if nothing unusual had ever happened. Solomon did not forget. He would never forget.

The lone figure remained standing by the graves as the wind howled around him, whipping his black trench coat around, until each button came unbuttoned slowly. If the weather bothered the figure, it was not noticeable.

He placed his hand gently on top of each gravestone of Sybil and Eric Tania. Then he sighed, turned and walked away. With the sigh came the knowledge that something was going to happen. Something big and astronomical! It was starting all over again. He could feel it in his bones.

△△△

A familiar figure walked through the glass double doors of the multi-leveled building. The title, *Project Interstellar* was prominent in bold sky blue letters over the portal. He smiled at everyone who greeted him and walked on toward the elevators.

There were several construction crews finishing up the last touches on the outside of the granite building. Solomon nodded as he walked by. The building sat on several acres of land on the outskirts of Seattle, Washington. The funding for *Project Interstellar* came from several prominent private citizens, along with some government grants. Opening day was a big deal.

Those who were involved kept a low profile for reasons of their own. The governmental funding came through an annual federal budget. The same one that funded NASA and various other agencies.

Most US space efforts had been led by NASA. The agency was also responsible for the Launch Services Program, which provided oversight of launch operations and countdown management for unmanned NASA launches. *Project Interstellar* was in that category. Solomon was excited about working there.

There were several NASA employees among the staff, which lent credibility to everything associated with the project. Solomon learned that the most notable among the NASA representatives was Colonel Andrea Sanderson. He was eager to meet her.

The thirty-five-year-old NASA veteran had been married to Major Jonathan Sanderson, who had died on one of the last shuttle missions. Despite the rumor mill, the blue-eyed, Brazilian beauty, who had long, curly, chestnut hair, was the one who paved the way for her husband to join NASA's ranks. Not the other way around.

Even though she was respected as an accomplished Aeronautical Engineer and the best in her field, Andrea was told by many people that she should have been a model. She said that this bothered her, because she thought she wouldn't be taken seriously. She was not just a pretty face.

Everyone showed her the utmost respect. When she went to work, she would put her long curly hair up in a bun and she didn't wear any makeup at all. She even lowered her voice to try to keep everyone's attention when she talked. They had to keep their minds focused on what she was saying, not her appearance.

She was credited with naming the new project. She proved that even though the companies goals were mixed between the stars and earth, hers were not. Anytime she would mention space, it would garner more attention and more funding. Solomon heard that her ideas were right on. He was impressed and looked forward to working with her.

ΔΔΔ

Professor Jeremy Ingram was named the project lead. Solomon was to meet him today.

Professor Ingram had been the head of the School of Environmental and Forest Services at the University of Washington for the past 20 years. Solomon looked forward to working under him on *Project Interstellar.*

In spite of being 54-years-old, he kept himself in amazing shape. He didn't believe in getting surgery or coloring his hair, so his salt and pepper hair and Van Dyke beard complemented his facial features. He had stunning hazel eyes and dimples that showed every time he flashed his smile. Those features earned him attention among the ladies.

He had been divorced for several years before deciding to take better care of himself. His last three wives left him because of his controlling nature. Everything had to go exactly as he deemed it should.

Ingram was personable when he had to be. Like when he was vying for more money for the university or meeting new colleagues who could benefit his career at some point. One colleague stated that his charm was downright contagious.

Although it was not his charm that won him the job of project lead. Instead, it was his knowledge and experience of not only the environment but also his love of space.

Ingram had degrees in forestry, astrophysics, and agriculture, as well as many decades of experience working with local environmental groups for protecting the planet.

He came up with several theories concerning the stars and planets having a direct effect on Mother Earth. He studied the moon and stars for years and the outcome they had on the earth, given the distance. He then logged information pertinent to proving his theories by running the idea by Colonel Sanderson. Several other astrophysicists at The National Aeronautics and

Space Administration (NASA) were on his team. They worked the surrounding areas.

NASA was the agency of the United States Federal Government responsible for aeronautics and aerospace research as well as civilian space programs. It focused on a better understanding of the earth through the observation system. It was established in 1978 by President Dwight D. Eisenhower.

Most US space explorations were now led by NASA, which are exploring bodies throughout the solar system with robotic spacecraft missions. Solomon believed to work for both systems was an honor.

Ingram would never state his hypotheses unless he believed beyond the shadow of a doubt that it could not be disproved. If it wasn't a fact, he did not even want to hear about it. For example, after researching astrophysics, he thought that the Big Bang theory made sense. So he believed it.

He was fascinated with the size of the universe. There were so many celestial bodies in the sky that it made one's head swim. Both the colonel and the professor did not believe in God. They shared the idea that the concept was developed by people who didn't have the knowledge to understand the science behind everything. Their shared beliefs and opinions were what brought them together.

Ingram handpicked his entire staff for the project and was given full control. Being a complete control freak, he would not have settled for anything less.

Once he was made the lead of *Project Interstellar*, he said he had to have the colonel by his side. He chuckled when he said that it didn't hurt that she was pleasant to look at as well. He obviously had a thing going on in his heart for Andrea.

There was only one God-fearing individual who Professor Ingram put on his staff. He was the man who made his way up to the top floor while whistling, "Amazing Grace."

Solomon Dancer.

CHAPTER TWO

Solomon had an ear-to-ear smile as he reported for duty on his first day.

He was not much for dressing in a suit and tie, but he knew how important the job was, so he compromised. He wore a gray pin-striped suit with a blue tie to match the sign out front. On the tie was a cross.

Taking the elevator up to the top floor, he stepped out with a spring in his step. Passing several office doors, he looked into a large meeting room separated from the rest of the level with bay windows. That was all there was to the top floor. All of the labs and research areas were located on the floors below.

Solomon walked with purpose, as he strode over to the office assigned to him. He looked at the name on the door and read aloud, "Solomon Dancer." He didn't really have a title, but that didn't matter for the moment. He never dreamed he would be working for anyone with connections to NASA. He smiled, let out a breath of air and opened the door.

He stopped in surprise when he saw Professor Jeremy Ingram sitting in the huge black leather office chair, behind the oak desk with a laptop on top of it.

"Professor Ingram!" Solomon exclaimed in relief and remembering to keep his Jamaican accent out of his speech. He had worked tirelessly on kicking the accent from his homeland because he was worried people would look down on him. "I didn't know you would be here today. Well, here meaning in my chair! Ha!"

Ingram smiled and calmly stood up. "I am sorry for the scare." His words were carefully chosen, so he spoke slowly and succinctly. "I always welcome new staff with a one-on-one hello. I hope I'm not keeping you from anything, Mr. Dancer."

Solomon shook his head and then the hand of Ingram. "No! Not at all. I was merely surprised because you were so quiet. Please continue to sit! I'll take one of these other chairs here."

Solomon sat down in one of the stationary black leather chairs in front of his desk. He did notice the name plate with his name spelled correctly on his desk. He breathed another sigh of relief.

"Please, call me Solomon. I don't believe in formalities."

"Alright, Solomon," Ingram replied with a smile. "That means that you may call me Jeremy."

"I don't know if I can do that, sir. You are the man in charge and deserving of respect."

"I appreciate that, Solomon, but I expect nothing less or in this case, nothing more. We're a team here. In spite of the fact that I am in charge, I want everyone to feel that I'm approachable. Please call me Jeremy. Everyone else does."

Solomon held his hands up, almost as if he was surrendering. "Okay. You win. I will do as you ask. Was there anything else you would like to talk to me about?"

Ingram stood. With his hands folded behind his back, Ingram walked to the window overlooking the grounds. "It's funny you should say that. I do have something to talk to you about." He then turned back to face Solomon. "I'm afraid I have some news that might be rather upsetting to you."

Solomon tried to keep his smile, but he remained nervous. The new job and all. It was all so overwhelming to him. "Whatever it is, I'm sure it will be fine."

Ingram forced a smile. "I have tried to come up with some personnel to assist you in your endeavors, but since we are a new organization, I don't have anyone to spare."

"That's okay," he said. "I know my business. Stars are just giant, luminous spheres of plasma."

Ingram grinned and nodded.

"There are billions of them in our Milky Way Galaxy. And then billions of galaxies in the universe. Who knows how many universes?"

Ingram put his hand over his mouth to smother laughter. "Sounds like space is covered."

Solomon breathed another sigh of relief. He tried not to expect the worst, but the situation was new. He kept his faith that with God everything would turn out alright. "That's not a problem, Profess... Jeremy. I had a small work area in my basement back in Portland where I worked by myself. I had papers everywhere, but that's how I stayed organized. I'm used to working alone."

"You'll be surrounded by people who can drop what they're doing and assist you at a moment's notice, Solomon. You mustn't hesitate to ask for help if you need it. I just don't have anyone available in your... specific area of expertise. I do apologize for this."

"Not at all," Solomon said, with a chuckle. "You have given me an incredible opportunity and I am glad that I have something that I can contribute to the project. Thank you very much for this chance to show you what I can do for you."

There was a slight sparkle in Ingram's eyes, and his smile widened. "It is definitely I who must thank you. You just might be the only person on staff who can understand what I'm trying to accomplish. It's your research into the Harvest Moon that drew us to you. The moon's connection to earth, along with making certain connections with astrology, that I find fascinating. Since I'm exploring a bold new world of finding the connection between our planet's environment and the alignment of the stars, your addition is invaluable."

"Thank you for your vote of confidence," Solomon replied, with a questioning look. "I'm not trying to be difficult, but I'm sure when you spoke of accomplishments, you meant all of us because I really appreciate being a part of a team."

Ingram glared at the tall Jamaican and lost his smile. "Yes, of course. You are correct, Solomon. It will be the goal of all of us. Not just mine. Not just yours."

Solomon couldn't help but notice the look of irritation that crossed Ingram's face. He'd learned an important lesson in those first few moments and that was that Ingram did not like being corrected. Something Solomon felt he had better remember.

"I will let you get accustomed to your new surroundings, Solomon," Ingram said coldly. "I do have other pressing concerns that command my attention, so I will leave you to your duties. I suppose you have the new employee manual with all of the numbers you might need?"

All Solomon could do was nod. He felt embarrassed.

"Good then," Ingram continued. "I will be in the research lab on the second level. There is one secretary for this floor. Her name is Tracey. Please feel free to introduce yourself. She is at the large round desk in the middle of the floor. She can help you out. I would introduce you, but duty calls."

As he talked, he spoke faster until the words almost ran together. Solomon assumed it was because his new boss was angry about being corrected. Solomon would definitely remember that.

△△△

Solomon was not as good a judge of character as he had been before. He accredited that to his new outlook on life. Thanks to God.

As he saw everything through new eyes, he wondered why it had taken him so long to devote time to the Lord. He had always known that God was out there someplace, but he didn't find Him to be a friend until he stood in front of the graves of Sybil, Eric and Isabella.

He stood in his now empty office and remembered all of the events that transpired back when they were all together. It was just a little over a year ago when he had lost his friends. He shook his head, thinking how close the world had come to the battle of Armageddon.

Solomon really believed that if it wasn't for Eric's prophetic dreams and sacrifice in the Middle East, the world would not still be in existence as they now knew it. It was a miracle.

He thanked God every day that he and his mother were still alive. It was the Lord who saved them. He enjoyed time in prayer with his Savior and studying the Bible more and more. It was how he learned more of God's ways, so that he might find wisdom from Him.

He carried a pocket Bible with him wherever he went and stocked Bibles in his car just in case someone wanted or needed one. He was always prepared. Each day, he would wake up, thank God for another day, and live it as if it may be his last. He was hoping that the gift of prophetic dreams Eric had would be somehow transferred to him so that he could have some kind of heads up when everything began to fall apart.

He even developed high blood pressure for which he was taking Lisinopril. That showed his weakness. He and his mother had long talks about his blood pressure. She tried to tell him that he needed to stop putting his life on hold and start living. She told him that when something happened, it would just happen. He could worry about it then. She was the one who talked him into taking the job with *Project Interstellar.* She told him he was brilliant and not to waste his intelligence. Thinking about her reminded him that he needed to call her. He promised he would call once he got settled.

The project supplied him with a new Samsung S6 smartphone, in case they needed to get a hold of him at a moment's notice. He pulled his phone out of his pocket and sighed heavily. He knew his mother was going to lecture him if he was still paranoid, but he couldn't lie to her.

He dialed her number and forced a smile, as he waited for the phone to ring. After several rings, he started to feel relieved that she might not be home to receive his call. Then he remembered that she never went anywhere.

"Good morning, my child," was finally the response on the other end. "I was wondering if you were going to call your mama on your first day of work."

"Of course I was, Mama," Solomon said while shaking his head. "I even called you before I got to meet with the secretary and discuss... stuff."

There was a brief moment of silence, then Calista spoke up. "You do... stuff, huh. Ha ha! You are so funny, child of mine! If you don't want to talk with me, or you are busy, I'll understand. You know that. Right?"

"No, Mama, I want to tell you about my work. I study the stars. They are so amazing. Since the dawn of time, stars have been a part of human life. Religions have been built around them. Astronomy is the study of the stars in the second heaven."

"I've heard of that."

"I study them." He clasped his phone tighter. "The telescopes here are so amazin'. Looking through them, we can study the laws of motion and gravity."

"Now that is a lot to study."

He told her how the invention of photography, the study of wavelengths of light, and motion of stars were all part of his branch of knowledge

"That's a lot to learn, son."

"It is, Mama. But I get a lot of money for it. Money I can use to take care of you." He told her how the Hubble Space Telescope being launched had provided the deepest and most detailed view of the universe. "Wish you could see it."

"Me too. So you know about all of that stuff?"

"Yes, Mama." He laughed. "I know all that stuff."

"I'm proud of you, Solomon."

He could not help but laugh. "Thank you for making me feel better. I can't understand why I'm so nervous. I know this job. I can do it in my sleep. But I'm still edgy."

"You're nervous because you were never paid for all of your knowledge before," his mother replied, with pride in her tone. "You can't know how thankful I am that God has shown you the way. Now you are getting paid for all of those smarts you were using for free. I am very proud of you, son. Your daddy would have been proud too."

Since he had been born out of wedlock, he preferred not to discuss his earthly father, so he ignored that part of the conversation. "I know you are, Mama. I am so glad you're still with me."

"Don't you go thinkin' that I'm going to the great beyond anytime soon!" She sniffed.

"I'm not, Mama." He smiled at the phone. "I am going to bring you to see me sometimes, so you can see the stars through the big telescope. Just might be on a night when the stars have a glittering collection. It will look like a fireworks show, with a burst of color on that night."

"How can that be?"

He told her how a cluster of stars is sometimes surrounded by a heavenly body of gas and dust. He explained how raw material forms a new star arrangement. Paths of star-filled clouds contain a cluster of stars—huge stars. "I wish you were young enough to bring you to look through the telescope."

"I got a lot of fight in these old bones and I am not ready to meet my maker yet. He's keeping me here, so that I can keep an eye on you!"

He ran one hand nervously over his bald head and took in a deep breath. He knew he had to be careful as to what he said to her. She was ready for a fight to prove her strength. "I know, Mama," Solomon finally said, calmly. "In fact, God could has chosen you to serve Him, as He did me. You'd probably do a better job. That's one of the many reasons why I need my mama. No matter where I go, I will always need you."

There was again a brief silence.

"Good answer," she replied. "I know you are all grown up and living alone, but my love follows you until the end of time."

Those last words made him slightly ill, as he was reminded about his task. He wasn't about to let her know what he was feeling. She had enough to deal with.

"I know, Mama," was all he could say at first. "I appreciate your strength and wisdom. I also know that even though I'm now in Seattle while you're still in Portland, it feels like you're right next to me with all the love I have for you. I do have to get started now, Mama. I love you and thank you for everything you did for me."

He could hear her sniffles on the other end of the line. He knew he touched her heart. All he did was speak the truth. He would have told her that Portland was not that far from Seattle, but he did not want to confuse her.

"Alright, baby boy," she responded, choked up. "You're the most precious piece of me that I brought into this world. I will always love you and worry about you. You know that. You're not going to stop your mama from worrying. You get on with your day and let me know how it went later."

"I will, Mama," he said as his eyes started to tear up.

"Bye, Solomon."

"Love ya', Mama. Bye."

CHAPTER THREE

Solomon approached the woman behind the round desk in the middle of the floor. She looked to be in her thirties, had short red hair, blue eyes, and did her best to cover up several freckles on her face with makeup. She had just gotten off of the phone, turned to face him, and smiled. "Good morning, Mr. Dancer. I take it your meeting with Professor Ingram went well?"

He smiled back but was caught off guard. "I guess you know everything that goes on here, Miss Tracey. Yes, it went well. Thank you."

"I know things before they happen, Mr. Dancer," she said confidently. "That's part of my job. Another part of my job is assisting you in any capacity that I can. I have extensive knowledge in PowerPoint, MS Word, Excel, and…"

"Whoa! I apologize for interrupting you, but I don't need to know your resume. If you are where you are, then you are here for a reason. I trust that you will be able the help me when I need it. I just wanted to introduce myself. Please call me Solomon, Miss Tracey."

"Thank you, Solomon," she returned, without losing the smile.

He started to walk away but then turned back quickly. "I have a feeling I will need your resources a lot, Miss Tracey. Let me know if I start to become a pest."

"You could never be a pest to me, Solomon," she replied, with a flirtatious grin.

ΔΔΔ

Solomon spent the day and a good part of the evening transferring all of his data on types of moons from a thumb drive to his new work computer. He knew that NASA shared data with various national and international organizations, which he would look into later. He was to focus on the harvest moon to do it now.

It took him quite a while—and a heavy investment in jump drives—to make the transfer. He didn't like the idea of storing in the Cloud or transferring from computer to computer, so he accomplished his task the long way, keeping it to himself.

He tried not to be the last person to leave the project that night, but he couldn't help it. He wouldn't leave until every last bit of data had been transferred. He made sure to get permission to stay from Professor Ingram, who was more than happy to grant the request.

Solomon had a lot to learn about the other employees, because he noticed that Stacey flirted with all of the men who worked on the top floor, just like she had with him.

He laughed at himself when he thought he might have had a chance to take someone out on a real date. His social life had been practically non-existent for quite a while now.

Stacey approached him before she left. "Are you sure you don't want to walk me down, Solomon?"

He smiled at her and sighed. "That is extremely tempting, Miss Stacey, but I really do need to complete this job before I can start any actual work. I should be finished in about a half an hour."

She frowned and pouted her lips in disappointment. He could tell it was just for show. "Alright then. Sam the security guard will let you out when you're ready. He'll be here all night long. I'll see you tomorrow."

As she sashayed to the elevator, she winked at him and then turned around to press the button to go down.

"Thanks for your help," he said.

After she left, he laughed and looked up toward heaven. "I know, Lord. I hope someday you might send me someone of the female persuasion, so I can have someone nice to take out. I don't necessarily need a mate at this time of my life, but a date would be great. I'm just sayin'."

He sighed again and went back to work.

△△△

It took him two more hours to finish the transfer. He had never typed so much in one sitting before in his life. His fingers ached and he thought he might have had carpal tunnel in both hands.

He glanced at the wall clock in his office, as he logged off his computer and shook his head. It was 10:26 P.M. He knew he had to be back at work at 8 o'clock the next morning. By the time he reached his new apartment, shook off the day, and got ready for bed, it would be close to midnight. *That's life in the big city.*

Solomon was satisfied with how much work he put in, though. There were some files that were written on a version of Microsoft Word that was much older than the version he had now. It took him a while to figure out the compatibility mode feature on the newer version. Once he did, he was on his way to success.

Having a feeling of accomplishment, Solomon closed his office door and walked slowly to the elevator. Once inside, he smiled, thinking about how fortunate he was to be involved with such an innovative company on the ground floor.

Once the elevator opened on the lower level, he heard what sounded like an older man yelling.

He looked around and didn't see the guard anywhere. Not near his desk nor near the front door. A feeling of panic set in. Solomon looked up in desperation as if to ask God for guidance. Almost as if on cue, the voice cried out again and echoed throughout the huge first floor. That time, he could tell exactly where it came from.

There was a waiting area just around to the right of where the guard desk was. It branched off into a small area, that was equipped with refreshments of all kinds.

Solomon ran toward the sound, pulled out his phone and immediately dialed 911. He needed to do that before he confronted whatever it was that was causing the man to scream like that.

"911. What's your emergency?" said the female voice on the other end.

Solomon looked up and saw that the glass doors in the front were shattered. He noticed that they had been broken before he had a chance to wonder about an alarm. He whispered, "I need to report a break in." His voice was raspy. "I am at the *Project Interstellar* building…"

"We know exactly where that is, sir," was the rushed reply on the other end. "Please stay calm and find someplace to hide until we can get there. Help is on the way."

He put his phone away and glared at the side of the wall where he stood. He was just a few feet away from trouble. He shook his head and understood that is exactly where he needed to be. Looking at it as a sign from God, he jumped forward, hoping to scare off the intruder and maybe save the guard at the same time.

When he landed in front of the melee, he saw a hooded figure accosting the older guard.

"Stop where you are!" Solomon shouted before he could figure out if the intruder had a weapon of some kind or not. He backed up just a bit as the hooded man's head jerked toward Solomon. He then ran toward the broken glass door.

Solomon rushed to the aid of the guard, who was lying on the floor, badly beaten and bloody. Solomon looked up and realized that the police wouldn't be there in time to catch the perpetrator. He checked the guard's pulse. When he realized that he was still alive with a good, solid pulse, Solomon told him to hold on. "Help is on the way,"

He then ran toward the broken glass doors, in pursuit of the intruder.

The hooded man was down the street, but still in his line of sight, so Solomon ran as fast as he could, trying to catch up with him. Though, he wasn't sure what he would do when he caught the guy. He would figure that out later. That wasn't his immediate concern. He had to stop the intruder at all costs, even if it meant his own life. As long as it spared someone else, it was worth it.

The figure dashed into a back alley, just as Solomon heard police sirens. He slowed down, knowing that someone had to be in the building to make a statement.

Solomon stopped right at the entrance to the alley and looked at the figure, who stopped at the other end of the alley and glared back at him. It was as if he knew he was no longer going to be pursued. There was a distance of about 100 yards between the two. They just stood there facing one another for several seconds, before Solomon saw the figure turn and take off running again. Solomon backed up slowly and then headed back to the building.

He heard the siren getting closer, meaning the police were approaching. He would show the officers which way the guy went. Perhaps they could catch him. He arrived at the building at the same time as the police and ambulance. He gave them the information as quickly as he could, in hopes that they could catch the person.

CHAPTER FOUR

After talking to the police, Solomon was required to be checked out by the paramedics, even though he insisted that he wasn't hurt. He kept focused on the direction in which the perpetrator had vanished, trying to resolve the issue in his thoughts. Nothing seemed right. There was no place to hide down there.

The police looked for him anyhow. After scouring the area for about an hour, the police returned, saying they could find no trace of him.

A paramedic told Solomon that the guard was going to make it, even with all of the blood loss. "The wounds weren't meant to kill, but incapacitate. The intruder knew what he was doing."

"That is good." So he was a man with a mission.

One of the officers said that the guard told him the intruder asked a lot of questions. It appeared that the guy was trying to interrogate the guard, but probably had no intention of hurting him the way he did. Solomon would remember that piece of information. He had a lot that he wanted to tell Ingram when he would see him the next morning.

△△△

When morning came, Solomon almost didn't get out of bed. He prayed for the mysterious man who attacked the project's security guard and hoped he would be caught.

All of the sudden, Solomon was bombarded with crazy thoughts regarding the end of the age. It started by his thinking about the intruder. Needing to rest his brain, he called the office and let them know he would be late to work, due to extenuating circumstances.

He took his time going to work, allowing time to think about the situation. Standing in front of the building that was to provide the means of a new start for him and his mother, he was confused. He hoped that if he could stay employed for any amount of time, he could move his mother out to live with him. Although, he was sure that the harder part would be convincing her to leave her home in Oregon.

Now he had the perfect argument for her. His first day of work turned out to be fairly dangerous. He was sure that would get her to move out there with him. The only problem with that was he would never hear the end of it.

He walked slowly into the building, and noticed that the broken glass door had already been replaced. As soon as he closed the glass doors behind him, everyone in the lobby turned and started to applaud. He even received a few whistles. He wondered if that was what it was like to be the hero. He didn't ask for the adulation, but got it, nonetheless.

As he walked toward the elevator, he simply smiled at each person who was giving him praise. He entered the elevator and assumed that would be the end of it. He was wrong. When the elevator opened on the top floor, Tracey and the other occupants of that floor were facing him and applauding as well.

Tracey had a small cart on wheels with a cake on it. It had a superhero on it with the word, congratulations on it. Tracey had an exceptionally big smile for him. Ingram rushed up to Solomon and shook his hand.

"Bravo, Solomon! Bravo! On your first day of employment, you managed to scare off someone we've been trying to catch!"

Solomon gave him a confused look.

Ingram turned to the others and said, "Everybody, please listen! Our hero and I have some very important things to discuss in private! Save the cake for lunch and please return to work. Thank you, everyone! I'm sure he more than appreciates the homage! Thank you!"

Ingram grabbed Solomon's arm and rushed him to the same office that he surprised the new employee in on the previous day. It was Solomon's office now.

Ingram closed the office door behind him and closed the blinds on the window. He then turned to Solomon with a huge grin. "You have no idea how long we've been trying to catch that person. We didn't even know that it was a man until you chased him. Bravo, again! That little deed of yours would surely be frowned upon, because of the inherent risk to life and limb. I, however, appreciate that kind of intestinal fortitude in my employees."

Solomon smiled and nodded. He didn't think he did anything special but refrained from mentioning that until he found out more about the intruder. Obviously, Ingram knew more about him than he was letting on.

"Thank you, Jeremy," Solomon returned humbly. "I believe the police were the real heroes last night. It was their sirens that chased the scoundrel away."

"Nonsense!" Ingram replied with a smirk. "You had everything to do with us getting one step closer to the saboteur."

"Saboteur?" Solomon asked, wanting to know more.

Ingram peeked through the closed blinds and sighed a breath of relief. "Good. Very few people know about what's been going on recently. Since you were directly involved, I can confide in you. Can't I, Solomon?"

Solomon nodded. "Of course, Jeremy. You can trust me, totally."

There was a strong knock on the office door, which didn't seem to surprise Ingram. He opened it to reveal a gorgeous lady. She was introduced as Colonel Andrea Sanderson. She stood almost at attention with somewhat of a grin. "Hello, Solomon," she said, sticking her hand out and firmly shaking his. "Glad you're on board. This project needs more people like you."

Solomon could tell that she was sizing him up with her eyes, to see if he was worthy to be working with her. "Thank you..." He glanced at Ingram and shrugged as if to ask him why the woman was important.

"Do you need something, Andrea?" asked Ingram.

"I have a question for Mr. Solomon."

"Ask away," said Ingram.

"You are the moon expert, aren't you, Solomon?" she asked.

"Some say that I am," said Solomon.

"Tell me, is there a correlation between a Harvest Moon and the moon's location in orbit?"

"Good question," said Ingram turning to face Solomon. "What do you say?"

"Well, The orbit of the Moon is distinctly elliptical, with an average of 0.0549 eccentricity. That is the non-circular form," Solomon said slowly. "A total lunar eclipse occurs when the earth aligns between the sun and the moon, creating a shadow. The astronomical term to describe this process is a Greek word which translates as being paired together. As we view the moon from earth, the moon appears to go through a complete set of phases, because of its motion around the Earth."

"That makes sense," she said.

"You might think the Harvest Moon is bigger or brighter depending on where it is in comparison as to where you are." He chuckled.

"That helps me understand."

"Your name is Andrea Sanderson," he asked. "Right?"

"Yes. It is nice to meet you."

"You too."

Ingram laughed and gently placed a hand on Solomon's shoulder. "I am so sorry, Solomon. I really am. I just assumed that Colonel Andrea Sanderson's reputation preceded her. Anyway, I guess you are to consider yourselves as just being introduced to each other."

She said, "I know all about you, my friend."

Solomon smiled. "Forgive me, Colonel Sanderson. I meant no

disrespect. I don't keep up with the news. That's my mother's job."

She acted like she felt more at ease with his response. "I think I'm going to like working with this one, Jeremy."

Sanderson sat down in one of the leather chairs in front of the desk. Ingram pointed to the other one for Solomon to sit in and he sat in Solomon's chair behind the desk once again.

Solomon wasn't sure if it was a power play to let him know who was in charge, or if it was just his natural way of doing things. Like he was naturally rude.

"Solomon," Ingram began, in a more serious tone. "Andrea is the only other person who knows about the attempts at terrorizing the project. There are factions who would love to see us fail in our endeavors. They are exceptionally clever at hiding from all kinds of surveillance and seem to have a learned where every camera in this building is. I don't want to think that someone internal is working both sides, but I may not have a choice. Each applicant and employee has been carefully screened through agencies that work closely with us." Ingram looked concerned.

"I am sure you will work it out, sir."

"Solomon," Ingram continued. "Since what happened last night... happened, I would like you and Andrea to work together on resolving this."

Solomon looked puzzled. He glanced at Sanderson and then Ingram, confused. "I'm sorry? I don't understand. I have no experience in these kinds of things. I certainly have no experience in detective work of any kind."

Sanderson said, "You just work on your project. I'll pursue the intruder."

"Of course." Ingram grinned. "Someone will try to steal your ideas."

Solomon shrugged his shoulders. "That is impossible. They can study the sky for themselves."

"Surely they won't understand the harvest moon." Ingram looked puzzled.

"True. That is my area of expertise."

"What is it that you are bringing to the table?"

Solomon explained that the greater thickness of atmosphere in the direction of a horizon scattered blue light most effectively, but it did allow red light to pass through to ones eyes. Thus, a moon near the horizon takes on a rustic hue."

"Interesting."

Solomon added, "It looks like autumn trees."

"I did not know that," Ingram replied. "You have done masterful work on your research into the Harvest Moon. I would even have to say, groundbreaking. You're the perfect person to team up with Andrea."

Sanderson smiled, smugly.

Ingram stared into Solomon's eyes with an almost crazed look. "Besides, this is right up your alley. We only have attacks on the complex during a full moon. In case you didn't realize it, last night's moon was also a Harvest Moon. Coincidentally, that was the closest the saboteurs ever came to causing real damage. I don't believe in coincidence. By the way. I... we believe that this group or faction is timing their attacks with the cycles of the moon. We need you to find out if that means something."

Solomon's eyes widened. Ingram was right. That was right up his field of expertise. "I don't get it. I must not have been paying attention to the moon last night because it really doesn't make sense." He thought about why it was different. "The orange color of a moon near the horizon has a true physical effect on the earth. That fact is rooted in how the horizon shows a greater thickness when the moon is full. Earth's atmosphere is more effected than when the moon is directly overhead."

"What doesn't that make sense?" Sanderson asked. "I don't understand."

Solomon walked over to the window and opened the blinds. He said, "The atmosphere has scattered blue light—that's why the sky looks blue. Isn't it beautiful?" He paused. "If there is supposed to be a Harvest Moon tonight, we should see some evidence."

"The moon tonight will be special, so we should enjoy it. The Harvest Moon gives an extra dose of lighting for farmers during harvest time. That is how the Harvest Moon gets its name. My concern is that this time, the full moon will behave oppositely. This could cause an extra length of time between the moon rising from one place to the next."

Sanderson said, "Is this moon really worth observing?"

"Definitely," said Solomon. "Any more questions?"

"No."

"No."

"May I be excused?"

"Certainly!"

"Then I will be going." He then bowed and excused himself from the meeting. He walked out the door humming "Amazing Grace."

CHAPTER FIVE

He believed he got out of there just in time. After Solomon asked to be excused from the rest of the private meeting, he went to his office to research all of his notes. He hoped Sanderson and Ingram would leave him alone to do his work. He wondered what he could learn new about back-to-back Harvest Moons, and if such a situation could cause harm to humans. After nearly an hour and a half, he gave up. No matter how hard he sought to find an answer, he found that he could not find one.

A knock on the door broke his concentration. "Yes, please come in."

Ingram opened the door and entered, followed by Sanderson. She looked impatient. Before he could say anything, she said, "I have been appointed to be your partner."

"Oh really?" He grinned. "Can you keep up with me?"

"Of course. I surpassed you a long time ago."

"Solomon," Ingram stated. "I know it must be frustrating to have an occurrence such as back-to-back Harvest Moons to cause havoc in your research, but I thought maybe Andrea can help."

"How so?"

"I know that the Harvest Moon is no ordinary full moon."

"True. It is going to behave kinda like a sunset for the next couple of days, which is a good thing for farmers."

"But bad for your project. Right?" He bit his lip.

"So that is why you're putting me on it," she snapped.

"No. You two figure it out." Without waiting for an answer, Ingram left the office, closing the door behind him, leaving an awkward silence that had already developed between Sanderson and Solomon.

Solomon sighed and leaned back in his chair with his fingers intertwined behind his head. He spun around a few times and let off steam by moaning.

Sanderson walked behind the desk and looked at the open computer. "I hope I'm not stepping on your male ego, but if I'm going to help, I need to see what you're doing."

"Really?"

The way she talked down to him made it evident that she didn't want to be there.

He inhaled deeply. "If you have pressing matters to attend to, I really don't mind figuring this out myself," he replied, with some aggravation at her attitude.

"You don't like me." She narrowed her eyes. "Is it because I'm a woman? Is that it?" she bellowed. "I have worked hard and for less pay than most men who don't know half of what I know or do half of what I do! You should be thankful that I even agreed to team up with you in any capacity!" She swore, her face turning red. "If I had the guts, I'd have..."

"Kicked my butt," he snapped back at her. He moved close to her, placing his finger on her nose. "But you didn't! Did you? And you're not going to, are you?" His patience had reached its limit. He didn't like allowing himself to be pushed that far, but he had to dissolve the situation before it became even more volatile.

She stepped backwards. "Don't touch me."

"I now know what you think of me." He did not move, but still faced her. "I wasn't sure if you didn't like me because I was new, but I believe that you hate everyone, equally! I have been given a job to do! As far as I can tell, you are not the one who hired me! Right now you are nothin' but a major annoyance, because it doesn't seem that you can work without bellyaching about something! I was actually looking forward to working with and learning from you, but I'm afraid that the only thing I could learn from you is how to be bitter at the world for something that just might be your fault!" He lowered his voice. "My mama taught me a long time ago to take responsibility for my own actions and not try to blame others when I fail! I mean no disrespect to your parents, but somebody should have taken a switch to you in your youth! Maybe you'd be a little nicer."

He walked over to the door, opened it, and held it open while he glared at her. He lowered his voice. "I ask that my God help me say this as nicely as possible, because I don't want to lower myself to yelling any more. Please, get out of my office and don't come back until you can be a civil, positive influence on the outcome of this research. Thank you and good day."

Sanderson stood for several seconds with her mouth hanging open in shock. She couldn't remember when she had ever been talked to like that, but for all intents and purposes, it seemed to work. She gave Solomon a puzzled look as he tried hard not to make eye contact with her. She slowly walked out the door. As much as he wanted to, Solomon did not slam the door behind her. He closed it gently, then leaned up against it in relief while shaking his head. As soon as she had exited his office, he could tell that she stayed in one position by the door, as if she was trying to comprehend what had just happened to her.

He looked up. "Dear God? I'm sorry. I know I will always be tested, but does it have to be a constant thing? I want to have patience and strength to deal with others. Please, help me, and be patient with me."

It was time to go to work. He needed to find dates and hours of all Moon phases during the present year. He knew that all dates and times are given both in Coordinated Universal Time (UTC) and America/Los Angeles Time Zone. Standard Time was normal. Of course Daylight Savings Time was a convenience for farmers. The Brown Lunation Number (BLN) was included for convenience. All seemed well. His project should work.

He opened his laptop and read about an ancient Mayan equinox celebration ritual. The sacrificial ritual was held by the pyramid at Chechen Itza, Mexico. He read, "The pyramid, known as El Castillo, has 4 staircases running from top to bottom of the pyramid's faces."

It was superstition. That would be his starting point the next day.

As he looked around his office, he wished that he had Sybil or Eric helping him. He missed his friends and hoped that they were with God. His heart was heavy as his eyes teared up, just thinking about them. *God rest their souls.*

A knock on the door startled him as he wiped the tears from his eyes. He turned and opened the door after composing himself.

Ingram stood there with a blank expression. "May I come in?"

"Please do. Come in, come in." Solomon nodded, as Ingram entered. Solomon closed the door. He quickly walked past his boss and took his seat behind the desk before Ingram could take it.

Ingram smiled. "Good. You're taking charge of your position and that pleases me. I can't stand weakness and besides me, you are the only one who has ever been able to put Andrea in her place. She has a way of intimidating those around her, to the point of tolerating her childish outbursts."

Solomon had a sick feeling, as he realized what was going on. "You think this is a game? People's lives are in jeopardy if the double Harvest Moon is what I think it is."

Ingram forced a smile. "Isn't life a game? It has challenges and competition throughout. You have to stay one step ahead of... well, everyone... if you want to succeed. Trust is not as easy to come by as it was decades ago. People are more self-serving and there are many things that help to promote that ideal. As a species, we claim we want the fairy tale ending and yet, we relish in the pain of others. We love to see our competition fall. Even those who we do not know must suffer so that we can feel better about our own pathetic lives. I would call you ignorant if you believed that there is anything outside of what we see is worth believing anymore."

Solomon stood proudly. "I believe in my Lord and Savior. My God in Heaven has strengthened me against the cruelty of this world. I have faith in things I cannot see with my physical eyes, but what I can see with my spiritual ones. I judge no one for how they see life and what they believe in. I am just proud to hang on to my beliefs no matter what happens to my flesh."

Ingram smiled again. "I wish I had your passion, Solomon. You passed again."

Another test? Solomon grunted. "I have to tell you, sir. Ever since I got here, not only has it been very crazy and fast-paced in this place, but I have been tested. Should not the tests have occurred before I got here? No! I know this is the way things are, but I honestly don't know how much more I can take. I need a break."

"Fair enough," Ingram responded, shaking his head like he did not know what he would say. "I will help. I promise you, now the tests are finished. Despite my university tenure, I have been involved in various business matters from time to time. I'm afraid I've developed a tough hide to go along with my distrust of the human race for the most part. I created some of these tests to put those I have already hired through the wringer, if you will. I feel that most people have their guards down once they have been hired, which makes it easier to test their true natures."

"I am today as I was yesterday. I cannot change that quickly and I wouldn't want to anyway. If we can get past all of this, I would like to hear more about this saboteur."

△△△

Solomon sat silently at his desk, staring at his stapler and wondering whatever caused him to get so overwhelmed.

"You okay?" asked Ingram.

"Yeah." His eyes softened. "What do you know about the intruder?"

It took Ingram a while to explain about the alleged corporate terrorism and the intruder. Abraham was surprised that Ingram didn't have any more information as to who was involved. Solomon actually supplied him with more information than he had before when he told what he knew about the moon. He said, "You know that a Harvest Moon qualifies as a super moon—the moon's closest point to earth for a particular month. The Moon will rise thirty minutes earlier, and then be full and close for a few days. We will experience it the day before and the day after the actual Harvest Moon. It seems to be magic to some."

Ingram said he found that to be fascinating, and assured Solomon that he didn't have to work on the special task force anymore with Sanderson. He gave him the choice of working on it by himself or just washing his hands of it altogether.

"I have found a connection to the past. The Mayans made notorious bloody human sacrifices connected to the full moon. They built a staircase at a carefully calculated angle which looked like an enormous snake of sunlight slithering down the stairs on the day of the equinox. I need to know more about it."

"Interesting. So do you think there is a supernatural component?"

"No, but some might."

"What do you want to do?"

"Right now I am leaning toward working alone."

At the same time, Solomon didn't want to take anything away from the experience that Sanderson brought to the table, but he figured he could do more to find things out by himself since he was going to approach it from a different angle. Ingram set things in motion when he removed Sanderson from the task of identifying the companies terrorist.

Solomon knew that would cause him to score even less points with her, but that was okay. He really believed he could find out more on his own. He would convince his boss that he had good ideas. He was getting Ingram's attention, and that would be a good thing if they became friends. After telling Ingram about his research, he saw that he was impressed. Even though the boss was close with Sanderson, he confided with Solomon that he didn't care too much for the way she operated or her attitude. If he thought Solomon did not need her expertise, he wouldn't have even considered her. He smiled. "Let's catch our intruder."

Solomon nodded that he understood. He wasn't afraid to do something that Sanderson frowned upon. He had a hunch and he was going to play it.

Since he figured out that the intruder made himself known during full moons and attacked during the Harvest Moon, he might actually be able to catch him that night. The Harvest Moons would appear to be on back-to-back nights.

△△△

Ingram walked out and Solomon got back to work. The name Harvest Moon was chosen because it appears in the Northern Hemisphere at the time of harvesting crops. It is at that time that birds migrate past the light that emits from the moon. That is important for the birds that rely on the moonlight to migrate from one area to another. They do no even begin their migration until they see the moon. He would ponder that one for awhile.

Ingram had made sure that a younger and stronger guard was going to be working that night when Solomon approached him with his plan. Ingram said he was excited at the possibility that they might catch the saboteur on Solomon's second night of work.

Solomon wanted Ingram to understand that everything had to look normal. As professional as that intruder was, he might have known if something or someone was out of place. Solomon was banking on a notion that the intruder might believe that the project wouldn't dream of being attacked for a second night in a row.

That's what made it so perfect.

Only a small group knew about the plan to potentially trap the intruder. This was a need to know operation.

Ingram wanted to leave a few lights on. One of them would be Solomon's office. Ingram sat in his newest employee's office and would walk around every once in a while, to give anyone outside the impression that Solomon was in his office. It would take him a few minutes to get to the ground floor if anything happened. At least that's the impression they wanted to give.

Solomon left his office earlier in the day and waited outside in a nearby van with several of the project's security force, watching on hidden cameras. Solomon couldn't believe how surreal his first two days of employment were. He then realized that he had turned his phone off. When he checked it, there were several missed calls from his mother.

He knew he couldn't call her yet, but he was going to be in trouble when he finally could.

As the sun started to set, Solomon waited impatiently. He was curious as to whether the second night of the Harvest Moon was going to be a night he would never forget. At gut level he believed trouble was coming.

△△△

Solomon and three guards were assigned the job of finding the intruder. The three security guards in the van focused their attention on the video monitors while Solomon glared outside of the van's windshield at the night sky. His heart raced as he saw the red glow coming off of the Earth's satellite. Shaking his head in disbelief, he looked down at one of the monitors, but saw nothing out of the ordinary.

He glanced over all of the monitors and then over to the guards who were showing signs of boredom.

"This is ridiculous!" exclaimed one of the guards in frustration. "Nothing's going to happen tonight! I'm going for snacks and coffee. Anybody want anything?"

The guards then showed signs of life, as they swarmed the idea of a man with food and drink. They placed their orders.

Solomon wanted to exit the van and stretch his legs, but he was told not to reveal himself.

After the guard took the orders, he looked at Solomon. "Do you want something?" All Solomon could do was shake his head. There was a tightness in his stomach that something big was going to happen soon. The red glow he saw coming off of the Earth's satellite looked closer. Solomon wasn't hungry or thirsty anyhow.

The guard just smiled and opened the sliding side door to exit the van. Right after he got out and closed the door, the van was knocked forward with a strong blast. It had been hit by something fast and heavy. An explosion caused Solomon to jerk to attention, Next, an eruption of a large smashing sound was followed by the van rolling over several times. Bodies rolled as well. The van became a death trap, since no one had seat-belts on. Electronic equipment shorted out and exploded, and metal pieces flew in all directions.

With glass and metal making the roll even more dangerous, Solomon just closed his eyes and held his hands over his head to protect it. He also said a silent prayer, but too much was happening too fast to protect anyone.

The van eventually came to a stop, landing with a direct impact. Solomon flopped down to the floor. He was just thankful to be alive. He heard a few groans. When he managed to open his eyes, he realized that the van was on its side. There was debris everywhere. The inside light on the top of the cargo area was blinking in erratic increments.

It seemed as if every muscle in his body ached and he felt a strong pain in his elbow and his right leg. He blinked to get a clearer picture of what had happened. He had an excruciating headache. He ran a finger along his forehead and looked at his hand. There was blood on his finger.

As he tried to move, he noticed that the other two guards were slowly coming around. "Please call the authorities," Solomon said.

There was no movement coming from the driver's seat. "Is… everyone okay?" he attempted to say, with his voice raised so that everyone could hear him. No answer. Solomon realized that they were in trouble.

"So far, so good," a voice finally said, and "yeah," was another weak response. Another said, "I called 911."

"Jamie's alive," a guard added, referring to the driver. "I don't know for how long, though."

Solomon could hear the sound of a large vehicle working its way to the project building.

Someone said, "It is the paramedics."

As Samuel worked his way free from the debris, he pulled himself to the new hole in the side of the van where contact could be made outside. Most of the metal was bent inward, so he had to be careful of the jagged edges.

"Jump now!" he called out.

CHAPTER SIX

*W*hat hit us? It was caused by the moon, he thought. *Noth-ing else could cause people to be that cruel.*

He felt it in his heart. A Harvest Moon had a strange effect on people. He looked up. The moon was full and visible. He realized that whenever the moon was full, it was near the horizon, like it had just risen. Solomon knew that the location of the moon in the sky was significant. When the moon was near the horizon, the Harvest Moon looked bigger.

Fear probably caused people to do stupid things. People were possibly scared for nothing.

He silently thanked God for sparing his life and the lives of everyone in the van, while adding prayers for the man they were looking for somewhere outside.

Samuel had to get out of the van. After navigating around the bent metal, he pulled himself up and out through a window opening. He sniffed the air and could smell gasoline. Poking his head back inside the van, he said, "You guys have got to get outta here! I smell gas and that can't mean anything good."

They showed fear. "How?"

"Climb out a window. Can you guys all get out on your own power?"

"Yeah," a male guard replied. "We should be able to get Jaime out too. You go find out what hit us!"

One guard jumped and another handed Jamie down. Soon all were free.

Solomon had been careful when jumping down from the van.

He put all of his weight on his left leg when he landed, which helped, but not that much. He rolled and then stood, slowly facing the building.

The glass door that had been destroyed and replaced in less than 24 hours, was once again shattered. He looked back to see the guards lifting Jaime out of the van, carefully through the same window he had just climbed out of. A female looked at Solomon and asked, "Do you want a weapon?"

Solomon started toward the building, shaking his head. "No, thank you. If I ever get into a situation that only a weapon can get me out of, then I don't think much of my chances to begin with."

He limped forward, without any regard to using stealth or being quiet. He figured that he was in no shape to be tangling with anyone in his condition, anyway. If they confronted him, he would try to use something they might not be prepared for.

When he reached the front door, he could hear the crunching of broken glass under his feet. All he could do was grimace. He surprisingly felt no fear. He attributed that to having the power of God within him. No matter what happened, God would guide him.

He walked into the building and looked around. As he approached the guard's desk, he saw that the guard had been beaten unconscious and was tied securely to his chair. "Anyone that can take this big guy out so easily is definitely not someone I want to be messing with," he said out loud. It was more of a statement to let the intruder know that he didn't want to fight, than anything else.

"Hello?" he bellowed through the empty ground floor. "I have no weapons!" He held his hands up as if to surrender. "I just want to talk!"

He stopped and listened to see if he could hear anything, including a response to his plea. He heard nothing, so he moved forward toward the elevator.

The lights flickered in the hallway near the elevators and the stairs. Solomon tensed, but didn't want to spook anyone. He heard the familiar ding of the elevator arriving at the ground floor and prepared to move fast.

As soon as he stepped on and pressed the button for the top floor, he realized just how vulnerable he really was. He assumed that the intruder would be on the top floor, since that was the only floor with the light on. He started to worry for Ingram's safety. He tried not to think that the saboteur would even consider murder, but he didn't know who he was dealing with.

The elevator stopped and he noticed the top floor button was lit up. He stood as close to the middle of the door as he could. He held his hands out to his sides and lowered his head to avoid eye contact. If he humbled himself in front of his opponent, then he thought he might have a chance of surviving the experience.

It appeared as if the elevator door opened in slow motion, and Solomon tensed in preparation for whatever would meet him on the other side of the door.

The door opened completely and Solomon had no choice but to close his eyes. He was waiting for something. Anything.

When nothing happened and he could hear no movement or anyone giving him orders, he opened one eye and slowly looked around. Nothing. No one. It was too quiet. Maybe the intruder was on another floor. He didn't believe that he could have evacuated so quickly. He then wondered if maybe he spent longer than he thought in the van.

Tracey's seat was empty. That was good. She would be safe.

He heard something like a thud coming from his office. Solomon shook his head, and he wondered why everything had to happen in his office.

He sighed, breathed deeply and slowly walked toward the only sound coming from the floor. His eyes darted quickly back and forth, watching for someone to jump out at him from behind a desk.

There was nothing but a scuffling sound coming from his office. It was also the only office with the lights on.

He hurried his pace, even though the pain in his leg was severe. He boldly grabbed the doorknob and turned it. Opening the door, he limped into his office but immediately froze.

He saw Ingram's still body on the floor. He didn't know if he was unconscious or something much worse.

Solomon crouched beside him carefully. Not only because of the pain in his leg, but also because he didn't know if whoever caused it was still nearby.

Checking to see if Ingram had a pulse, Solomon let out a small groan of concern. When he did, he saw the curtain by the window move slightly.

He wasn't much of a fighter, but it was apparent that he had enough of the craziness that happened over the last couple of days. He gritted his teeth and looked around for some kind of weapon. He saw nothing, so he picked up one of the smaller chairs he had in front of his desk and walked slowly toward the window.

He stopped when he saw the curtain move again. That time, he was sure the window wasn't open just like he assumed earlier. Something was making the drape move.

He let out a primal yell, as he propelled the chair toward the window with all of his might. He almost fell forward but managed to catch himself on the corner of his desk, as he watched the chair sail toward the window.

When the chair burst through the window, a figure darted out from behind the curtain. As the chair crashed through the window, it became entangled in the curtain and dragged it down to the parking lot below.

The figure rolled on the floor and practically bounced back up to his feet. He had on a long, black trench coat and wore a ski mask covering everything on his face except for his eyes. He narrowed his eyes at Solomon.

Then, in total surprise to Solomon, the man's eyes widened, and he started to back up against the wall. He quickly eyed the door to the office and rushed to it. Solomon wasn't about to let the intruder get away again. He was prepared to make sure that he was put behind bars.

He dove for him before he could make it out the door. He stretched out his left hand and grabbed the cuff of the intruder's jeans. He held on for dear life.

"Not this time, you don't!" Solomon exclaimed as the man kicked at the new project employee with his free leg.

One of the wild kicks managed to connect with Solomon's forehead, which caused him to let go of the pant cuff. The man then sprang to his feet and ran clumsily out of the office and toward the elevator.

"No!" Solomon shouted, as he too rose and ran after the man. The pain in his elbow and leg only fueled his anger and made him run faster and harder.

The intruder looked back several times with fear in his eyes, which slowed him down considerably. It inspired Solomon to run even harder.

The man pushed the elevator buttons continuously as if that was going to make the elevator magically appear and save him. It was obvious that he wasn't going to make it.

The man braced himself as the doors to the elevator finally opened. Just as he tried to duck inside, Solomon slammed into him and knocked him backward, falling on top of him. The door closed and Solomon put all of his body weight on top of the man to pin him, but he was wiggling around so much that Solomon slid off him. As he did, he banged his head against one of the hand rails. While Solomon rubbed his head, the man climbed onto the rail and pushed the trap door overhead. Solomon regained his senses and grabbed the man's leg, holding on tight, grunting various verbal sounds.

The man struggled to get free, but Solomon's grip was like a vice. The frustration was obviously building for the intruder, as he was frantic to escape, but couldn't. Then something unexpected happened.

"Let me go, Solomon!" spurted out of the intruder.

Shocked, Solomon let go. Not because he was told to, but because the intruder knew his name. Furthermore, he recognized the voice.

The intruder stopped struggling, as Solomon narrowed his eyes on him. He jumped down to the floor of the elevator and pressed the red button, which stopped mid-floor.

Solomon stepped closer, making sure to be careful in case there were any more sudden movements. There weren't. All fight had left the man who had been evading capture for quite some time. He looked tired and was even breathing strangely under the mask.

"Do I know you?" Solomon asked, hesitantly. He knew he recognized the voice. He just couldn't place it. "You might as well speak to me now, because it will be too late later."

The man silently paced in the small area he had. "Alright. I had no idea that you were going to be here. Actually, I did have an idea, but now I think it was just a plot to lure me in. Not the idea, but you being here. I really believe that you were hired to trap me. I think that idiot in the other room knew more than he let on. I don't understand how he could have known and not come after me. It's nice to see you again, by the way. I feel really stupid, but I couldn't have just looked you up after all this time."

Eric?

"You are different," Solomon said, in a quiet voice. "You're supposed to be dead. Either your spirit has not been released to eternity or you were never in the casket."

The man laughed. "I am alive and standing right in front of you."

"No." Solomon had enough and reached over and grabbed the ski mask off the intruder. Solomon fell to his knees with his mouth open in disbelief. "What the heck! Why have you returned? You can't be alive."

This had to be the soul of Eric. His soul was a little thinner than Eric had been and he hadn't brushed his hair in a while, but the intruder had to be the returned soul of Eric Tania.

"Nice to see you, Solomon. Did I say that already?"

"No. Couldn't have."

"By the way, the world that we helped save a year ago is still around. The *Project Interstellar* is accountable. The guy who hired you will be responsible if it blows up."

"I still have time to figure it all out. I know that the moon during the year rises about 50 minutes later each day. Time shortens to 30 minutes near autumn equinox. We'll see an array of colors not seen otherwise. We will have some extra time between dusk and dawn. That should be what saves us," said Solomon.

"Why are you here? What is your goal?" asked Eric.

"I've been asked to study the moon to see how it affects things like wildfires in North America and dust storms in Africa." If this was not Eric, then Solomon felt weird talking to a spirit.

Eric frowned. "There is a moon illusion when the moon looks bigger, but that should not make any difference with your research."

"True." Solomon felt like he was on to an answer. "I'll tell you what I am going to do. I will watch for a low hanging harvest moon."

CHAPTER SEVEN

Solomon needed time to think. He crouched down for several minutes with one hand on the rail and the other on the floor of the elevator, to prevent himself from falling over. He still couldn't process everything he had experienced over the past hour.

Eric Tania had supposedly sacrificed himself along with Isabella to prevent the end of the world last year. Either he had not sacrificed himself at all or he had not yet gone to his final resting place. Which was it? He didn't think he was going to get the entire story from Eric in the condition he was presently in, but he also knew that he had to try.

He knew that there was no way Eric could have worked alone. He had not remained hidden by himself. He had an assistant. He also believed that Eric's accomplice might have been the one driving whatever vehicle had crashed into and overturned the van.

He needed answers, but he also knew that the inside of the stopped elevator was not the place he would have the time to get them.

"Eric," he said quietly. "We need to go somewhere so that we can have a nice, quiet place to talk. I really need to know what has happened to you. Why are you here? Where have you been for the last year? I need you to tell me."

"Yeah, yeah, yeah!" Eric responded with restored fervor. "I have a place. A couple of places, actually. I have to check with my buddy before making any plans."

Solomon forced a smile. "I'm your buddy too, Eric. Aren't we still buddies?"

Eric paused and then smiled. "Hey, yeah! We are buds! Cool! I can take you to my Bat Cave then! Boy, are you gonna love it there!"

"Sure! Okay." He held up his hand. "Listen. What's that noise?"

Solomon could hear the sound of several people entering the building and not being very quiet about it. He knew it was the authorities. He couldn't let them catch Eric just yet. He had to find out all he could. Especially the part about Ingram somehow being involved in a plan to wipe-out the world. He knew that if he helped his friend, he would then be wanted by the law as well. Unless he could find a way to make sure that no one knew he was helping. Or if Eric was just a spirit, then no one else could see him.

Then Solomon had a scary realization. "Oh, no. There's video of everything that has gone on here. I am so out of a job. I might as well give myself up now because they have me dead to rights."

Eric laughed loudly, as he pointed at Solomon. He then stopped and started again, as if he had a secret. "Do you think that my other buddy wouldn't have thought of that? Hah! You would be seriously wrong if you thought that! Seriously! Nope. All is taken care of! Ha ha!"

Solomon gave Eric a puzzled look. "So, everything that happened over the past couple of hours is not really on video?" He tried to put it in as simple terms as he could so that Eric wouldn't have a problem understanding him. Just in case.

Eric couldn't stop nodding. "Yep, my buddy. All taken care of. Didn't I just say that? Was it out loud or did I just think it?"

"Out loud." Solomon stood up and approached Eric, slowly. "Eric. There are people who want to arrest us just outside and probably a floor down from where we are. I don't think we can go that way. Do you and your other buddy have another plan to escape, in case the front and back doors are cut off?"

"Heck, yeah!" Eric answered while looking around the elevator. He then smiled, stared at Solomon, and used his index finger to point up.

Solomon sighed. "That's where you were trying to get to, when we struggled. So we need to climb to the roof?"

Eric leaned in close and whispered. "Yes, sir. That is exactly what I'm talking about. If we don't hurry, we are gonna be locked up for a long time and then my buddy won't be able to help us anymore. We have to go up."

△△△

It took some convincing for Solomon to climb through the opening in the ceiling of the elevator, and out on top. It wasn't easy for him, because of how tall he was, while Eric climbed up like a monkey. He moved fast and was sure of himself, like he had practiced his moves several times.

Once on top of the elevator, Eric replaced the cover and looked up. "I'll climb up and throw you a rope down, unless you'd rather climb up the same way I do. If so, then you can just follow me," he said.

Solomon shook his head. "I'd rather climb a rope, but how can you lift me? I am bigger than you."

"Don't worry about the small stuff," Eric replied, with a gleam in his eye. His confidence, made Solomon feel slightly more assured.

Without another word, Eric grabbed the thick cable and proceeded to pull himself up, as he used his legs to wrap around the cable to prevent himself from slipping. The muscles in his upper arms stood out and Solomon saw that he had trained hard for his mission of trying to destroy the project. Someone wanted the project to fail at all costs. They obviously put a lot of thought and planning into it.

A few seconds later, the end of a rope fell at Solomon's feet. He grabbed it, looked up and gave the rope a tug, to make sure it could support his weight. Even with all of the new idiosyncrasies that Eric was exhibiting, Solomon still felt that he could trust him completely. He wrapped the rope around his hand and tried to climb it. Obviously, he didn't have the kind of upper body strength that Eric did, so it was hard.

"Wrap your foot around the rope and do the same thing with both hands!" Eric's voice echoed through the elevator shaft.

Solomon winced, thinking that the police would find him for sure. He quickly did what he was instructed to do and inhaled deeply. "Okay!" he yelled back.

The rope started to move slowly upward at first. Then, it picked up speed to move at a steady pace.

Solomon was up to the top of the shaft in no time. He noticed some sort of mechanized system that appeared to have been there for quite some time. There was a small passage to either side of the huge metal bars that ran across the top. Solomon saw that the elevator could only go so far underneath the bars. There was plenty of room for several people to navigate through.

Eric disappeared down the darkened corridor, leaving Solomon hanging. He tried to swing the rope and managed to make it move just enough so that he could get his foot on the nearby ledge. After struggling with trying to pull himself over with just his foot, he made it and timed it just right so he could let go of the rope and land with half of his body in the corridor.

He had to almost crawl through the darkness, wishing he had a flashlight. He felt a bit of a chill, as he realized that the night sky was overhead. He stretched upward and looked at the stars, millions of stars. He realized that his light source was the moon, the beautiful Harvest Moon. He then saw Eric standing near the edge of the building.

"Time to go, man," Eric said, quietly for the first time. "Down this way." He pointed down.

Solomon walked cautiously over to where Eric was and glanced down without getting too close to the edge. He saw a mattress on top of what appeared to be a van. At second glance, it might have been an air mattress.

"No," he said, without thinking, as he turned toward Eric.

Eric shrugged with a half-smile. "Suit yourself, buddy." He then jumped over the edge of the roof and landed on top of the air mattress. Once he hit, he rolled off and onto the concrete alleyway. He popped up holding his shoulder. He looked at Solomon. "It's our way or their way," he said, pointing out to where Solomon could see the reflection of all of the red and blue lights coming from the front of the building.

Eric climbed into the passenger side of the van. Soon afterward, Solomon could hear the side door sliding open. It was a good thirty feet, easily. Solomon thought about the consequences of not following Eric. He thought about being wrestled to the ground and taken to jail with no bond. He also thought about how Ingram would be so disappointed in him that he would make sure Solomon would stay in jail—a long time. He had the resources to do it.

The van's engine started and Solomon knew that Eric's buddy was driving. Taking several deep breaths, he prepared to jump. His curiosity had gotten the better of him, but he needed courage. Looking up toward heaven, he prayed. Taking several deep breaths, he believed he had connected with God. So he jumped.

CHAPTER EIGHT

As Solomon fell, he subconsciously tried to reach out for something to break his fall. He landed with a significant thud on the mattress instead. His momentum caused him to roll off, just like Eric. He hit the ground but did not pop up as quickly as his friend had. He groaned as he managed to stand and fall forward—into the van through the open side door.

"Cool, Solomon!" Eric exclaimed from the passenger seat. He pointed to a bungee cord, "Release that cord there and the mattress will fall off. Can't go driving around town with an airmattress on the roof of the van. Kinda conspicuous, right. Haha!"

Solomon was dizzy and felt a sick tightness in his stomach. He wanted to get off the crazy ride he was on. *What am I doing?* He unhooked the bungee and whipped out of the open door releasing the air mattress.

"I never expected you to be on our side," said a familiar voice from the driver's seat. Another familiar voice. "If I would have known that you and Eric knew each other, I would have approached you before Jeremy got a hold of you."

He thought he was going to pass out with everything he had been through recently and almost did, but hearing the voice made him hold on to consciousness so he could identify who it belonged to.

The van moved out slowly, so as not to draw any unwanted attention and the mattress slipped right off of the top. They drove for what seemed like a good half hour until the van stopped.

"I wish you would say something, Mr. Dancer," the voice said, with almost a sense of urgency. "You're starting to freak me out."

Eric was abnormally quiet, as he looked out the window and hummed an unrecognizable tune.

"I'm sorry," Solomon said. "I do know you. Don't I?"

"You don't recognize my voice?" the driver replied, with a chuckle. She took off the seat belt and turned to face Solomon. It was Colonel Andrea Sanderson. "Do you remember me now, Mr. Dancer?"

"Oh my gosh."

ΔΔΔ

Solomon was in complete shock as the van bounced over a rugged path and guided them into what appeared to be an abandoned warehouse, several miles outside of the city limits. There were several *condemned* signs all over the structure and the surrounding area.

Eric and Andrea traded places. As Eric drove the van into a different section of the warehouse, Sanderson said, "We need to get out Dancer."

She took Solomon through a small entrance in the back, where there was no door. Rather, a part of the aluminum wall slid to the side to reveal a much bigger surprise.

Sanderson left him at the entrance to what he assumed was some kind of huge telecommunications center, equipped with state-of-the-art computers, surveillance, and several other forms of technology that looked too advanced even for the *Project Interstellar* to own. He glanced at a couple of the monitors and noticed that they displayed various areas from the inside of the project building.

He was shocked to see that it was occupied. Many people were rushing from one area to another. Some had headsets on and appeared to be talking to someone, while others were frantically entering data into computers and checking into other devices. Solomon was overwhelmed.

To one side was a set of wooden stairs that appeared to lead to an upper office. He surmised that the warehouse was once used for some kind of production of a certain product, because he saw boxes piled up in one corner with the words, *Summer's Peaches*.

He stood perfectly still, expecting to wake up from his dream any minute. His fear was that he would be sorely disappointed when he realized that it was no dream. It was actually happening. He was living in a real nightmare.

Sanderson returned to Solomon, placing her hand on his shoulder. She wore a black jumpsuit and black tennis shoes with matching gloves. Her hair was pulled back into a bun as usual and she still wore no makeup. He looked into her eyes and felt a twinge of fear.

"Are you alright, Mr. Dancer?" she asked, with an unsure look as to whether she should tell him anything more.

"No, I'm not alright," he answered, looking around the room and then ending up glaring at her. "I don't believe I will ever be alright again. I don't know what to make of all of this. One thing I know for sure. Eric is dead. I paid to have his body moved here in the States."

She smiled and said, "Follow me." She then headed past all of the people and machines on the floor and headed straight for the stairs. When she reached the base of the stairs, she turned to look at him once more. As he approached, she opened the door to the office, which had a huge window overlooking the floor below. She entered and sat down behind her desk. There were several plaques and pictures from NASA on all the walls. Solomon entered, looked around, and slowly sat down in the wooden chair in front of her desk.

"I'm sorry," he said, still in a daze. "Do you want me to close the door?"

She shook her head. "There's no need, Mr. Dancer. I have nothing to hide from the people down there. It appears that I have nothing to hide from you anymore, either."

He sat on the edge of his seat, filled with desperation. He needed to have answers to his questions, so he could make sense of everything happening around him. "Please tell me what's going on. I don't know if my mind can process all that has happened in the past few days, but I need to know. I thought I was getting the opportunity of a lifetime, not a trip into the Twilight Zone."

Sanderson laughed as she leaned back in her chair, interlocking her fingers in front of her waist. "I know you have a lot of questions. Why don't you allow me to explain first, and then you can ask about anything I don't cover."

He nodded in agreement.

"Good," she replied, with a firm tone in her voice. "There's a small refrigerator filled with bottled water behind me to your left. If you get thirsty, help yourself. You don't have to ask." She cleared her throat. "Let me begin by saying that I am in charge of the Seattle chapter of an organization that I guarantee you've never heard of. We're the *Global Peace Initiative* or the G.P.I. for short."

Frowning, he shook his head. He looked out the window and then sat back in his chair.

She continued, "We were originally set up by some extremely wealthy people in 1960 because they didn't believe that the U.S. government had the right ideology to lead this country into prosperity. President John F. Kennedy was one of the founding members." She lowered her voice and her words trailed off; then she said, "Now you see why he was really assassinated."

Solomon rolled his eyes and groaned.

Returning to her speech, she said, "Unfortunately, because the organization was still new at the time, the plan was found out. The rest is history. Now it is all different. Certain people want you to now know what is going down."

Frown lines formed on his brow. Solomon had looked on in disbelief until now. He hoped there was some way she could prove whatever she was talking about, but said nothing.

She sighed and sat up straight in her seat. "We don't have accurate records from that time, but I can assure you that the facts are true. The organization wants nothing more than to reveal the lies and bring to light the truth to anyone who will listen.

There are still many prominent members who have taken extreme measures to keep our activities hidden. Some have notions regarding our existence, but we are very good at covering our tracks."

"If I may?" he interrupted. "I know you said you would answer all of my questions later, but I really must ask at least this one now."

She nodded. "Go ahead."

"Where does Eric fit into this?"

She grimaced. "I was going to get around to him later, but I suppose I'll answer that one now. We followed your exploits concerning the Blood Moons last year. That was when we met Eric and learned of his dreams. When we were able to talk to him, he was more than willing to sacrifice himself for our cause, but when we learned about his dream machine, we assumed that his connection to what was going on was bigger than any of us had realized."

"Oh yes, he had supernatural dreams." Solomon walked over to the refrigerator, grabbed himself a bottle of water, then returned to his seat. "I had almost forgotten about that."

She waited for him to sit back down, then continued, "I'm not a big believer in the supernatural. In fact, I'm not a big believer of much that I can't see in front of my face. Never-the-less, we retrieved the record of his dreams from Dr. Seymour Caladasian. Very nice little gadget he had, but money talks and it's in our possession now."

Solomon remained expressionless, as he took a sip of water.

Sanderson cleared her throat and looked abnormally relaxed. More so, than when he first met her. "When we recruited Eric, he was more than willing to join our cause, but felt that he should have the appearance of sacrificing himself. That is what went down."

"He faked his own death?"

"Yes."

He frowned. "Interesting!"

"It took some convincing on his part, but we told him that we would eventually recruit you, as well."

"You were *pretty* sure of yourself," Solomon said, with some disdain.

She grinned. "We try to be as prepared as we can for as long in the future as we can. Yes, you could have said no. You can still say no, Mr. Dancer."

"You can call me Solomon."

"Okay Solomon."

"What happens to me if I say no?" he asked, with some trepidation. "Do I disappear because I know too much now?"

"No, Solomon," she responded with a laugh. "We are not a terrorist organization, nor are we the mafia. That's not how we work. We would simply erase your memory from the moment that you found out Eric was alive and dropped you back off at the project. It's a safe procedure. We have a 100% success rate."

"Let me get this clear. Are you saying Eric never died?"

"That is right."

"Are you sure we are not dealing with his spirit?"

"I don't know that part for sure."

"Who is in his casket?"

"It was just dirt."

"He is so opposite of what he used to be." Solomon took another sip of water. "Why is he... like that? I mean, when I knew him, he was very different."

"I knew you were going to ask about him," she answered reluctantly. "Once we recruited him, we needed to use the dream machine on him. At first, there was little to no effect. After several uses, he started to display a distinct hyperactivity and resorted to what we can only decide is almost juvenile behavior. Before you blame us, remember one thing, Solomon. You admitted that you are having trouble grasping everything that has happened over the past several days yourself."

"True."

"Add to that what you went through last year, and you would be a prime candidate for this kind of mental regression."

Mental regression. He shivered.

"The strain of Eric losing his sister, prepared him to want to sacrifice himself. Plus losing Isabella, whom he was growing quite fond of, was enough to push him over the edge."

Solomon felt rage. "You are using him."

"Not really. He still holds onto previous knowledge and can distinguish who his true friends are. He even holds onto the belief that God is actually an entity who protects the faithful."

Solomon tightened his lips. "He is not the only one who believes in God, Andrea. I believe with all of my heart because I have seen His work. I will not judge your beliefs and I expect you to return the favor."

"Fair enough," she returned, with a slight smile. "I'm sure as a student of the stars, you've seen many strange occurrences that even the best scientists can't figure out. I'm also sure you're not ignorant to all of the bizarre weather patterns and natural disasters that have been appearing in places never before seen until recently."

"Yes," he answered with a sigh. "I keep up on all of the natural and unnatural phenomena concerning the stars and planets and how they affect our planet. Eric, Sybil, and I were sure that the end of the world was going to happen last year. It was weird. Now I look at the moon from a biblical point of view. Try looking at the moon tonight as being created by God when it's rising in the east. You might notice something different."

"How so?"

"The low-hanging moon will look very big. This is a trick of the eye known as a moon illusion. It makes me think about God."

"You're joking."

"It shows we are at the end of this age."

"I've heard that not even the angels in heaven know the end time," she said, with confidence. "Before you say anything about that to workers, allow me to research all belief systems. I'll see what they have professed and if it has some basis for truth."

"Sounds fair."

"As a scientist, I have to know something exists, before I can add it to my own research or dismiss it."

"That's impressive," he added.

"Why does it seem impressive to you?" she miffed back. "Is it because I'm a woman and can't be impressive unless I'm normally showing a body part?"

His eyes bugged out. "What? That is what you said before."

"Never mind. I don't want to know the answer. I obviously digressed from the topic."

"It is because you are human with human urges." He winked.

Clearing her throat, she composed herself to continue. "I'm sure you noticed the back-to-back Harvest Moons."

"Yes," Solomon replied. "In fact, I have never seen a recorded incident of it ever happening like what is going on now. There is no scientific explanation that I know of and there is also no Biblical explanation either."

"Exactly!" she exclaimed. "So if it's not scientific and it's not Biblical, what would you say that it is? Let's rule out magic, if you don't mind." She rolled her eyes at the latter.

He chuckled. "I don't believe it's magic," he said firmly. "The only rational explanation left would be man-made."

"Bingo!" she returned enthusiastically, with a gleam in her eye.

"That's impossible!" he replied. "You are now talking about some kind of science fiction! We don't have that technology that I'm aware of! Please, tell me that we don't have that kind of technology!"

She narrowed her eyes at him. "I don't believe we have that technology either, Solomon. I work at NASA for a reason. My parents were members of the original formation of the group and trained me from childhood to be as knowledgeable as I could be about organizations that take control. I met Jeremy early on in my career because it was evident that his course was already predestined. I know for a fact that NASA doesn't have anything that could be sent into space to give the illusion of a Harvest Moon. *Illusion* is the key word here. I'm sure you're also a student of human nature to some degree. How gullible would you say the human race is at the present time?"

Snickering, he thought about it for a moment and wondered if it was a trick question. He shrugged his shoulders. "They are extremely gullible. We are too quick to believe whatever those in power tell us because we feel that they are the most informed. For some reason, we would never think that they would lie to us. I'm no psychologist, but maybe it's because we want to believe that we wouldn't be lied to. By those over us."

She smiled, as her features softened. "Right again, Solomon. It doesn't take a PhD to figure that out. All you have to be is perceptive to your surroundings and to people. Our organization is filled with people who are that perceptive. That's why it's important to add your knowledge. Jeremy has deceived people into believing that the Harvest Moon has appeared on back-to-back nights for a reason. For those who rely on science, what do you think are the odds that something like that would be?"

"That includes those who know the Bible as well."

She agreed.

He thought about his answer. He was starting to see why the G.P.I. was so important, if it was everything she said it was. "Chaos," he finally answered. "It would be utter chaos because there is nothing about it in the Bible and I'm sure that there is nothing to prove it in science. People will panic."

"Do you remember the radio broadcast many years ago during the last World War, Solomon?" she asked. "Even though they ran a disclaimer every so often stating that it was just a radio show, more people than not panicked. They rioted. Do you remember everyone panicking in 1999, because they thought that all of our technology would crash once the year 2000 hit? Like they actually believed that the tech giants weren't prepared for it. Bill Gates made another fortune selling Y2K kits to fix the problem. The kits were a placebo for a society with an overactive imagination. If there's no record of back-to-back Harvest Moons happening, then Jeremy is creating his own little Y2K scare, amplified about a billion times."

Solomon's eyes widened. "That is going to send everyone into a worldwide panic! People everywhere will think it's the end of the world!"

"Right. I'm glad we're on the same line of thinking, Solomon. We have to find some way to not only find out how Ingram is doing it but stop him without revealing our organization. The public has to believe that this went away on its own. If it came out that someone helped to prevent the end of days, then they will still be primed for another attempt at ending the world. Knowing what you now know, I have one more question for you. If people are starting to panic now, what will they do when the Harvest Moon is seen seven days in a row?"

CHAPTER NINE

Solomon chose to be on board with Sanderson, but he needed to pray for guidance. He also needed to keep his eyes open, just in case Sanderson was lying to him. He hated being paranoid, but he had to do the right thing. He needed wisdom, so he prayed intensely for clarity. He knew that making decisions when he was confused was not the right thing to do. He needed to be calm. He would mull the facts over in his mind as he knew the what to do.

He returned to his office the next morning. He sat quietly with his elbows on his desk and his head in his hands. He enjoyed the quiet but still thought that he was forgetting something. He let his mind roam. Then that something presented itself to him.

His phone rang. He had it set on vibrate while at work, but he could feel the vibration on his hip. It startled him back to reality and he grasped it quickly. His heart sank as he saw who was calling him—someone he hadn't talked to in several days. His mother.

He quickly answered the phone. "Mama! First, let me apologize for not getting back with you. I…"

"I may be old, but I am far from stupid, Solomon," she interrupted with a calm demeanor. "I know you're an adult and don't have to call your mama every day. Unless you love her, that is."

There it was. The guilt.

He closed his eyes and tried to breathe regularly. "You know I love you, Mama. It's just that I'm caught between the proverbial rock and a hard place right now and I'm having some trouble making a decision."

The other end was quiet for a few seconds and then she spoke in her sweetest voice. "Now, baby. You know I could have helped you with whatever it is that's making you crazy. God can help you more, of course. Since I don't know what the problem is, let me help in another way."

He listened intently and with some curiosity. It wasn't like his mother to completely try to take over his problems. "I could use your wisdom," he managed, after trying to think of the perfect thing to say to satiate her.

"Of course you can," she replied without missing a beat. "No matter what you're going through, it always comes down to what's right and what's wrong. Sometimes, we want something so much that we try to convince ourselves that's the way we should go, when it really isn't. Other times, we are caught like a fish in a net, between two friends or loved ones who are pulling on us like we are the rope in a tug o' war. Still other times, we can't tell which decision is the right one and which one will lead us down the path to evil and sin. I know you prayed about it. That's the best thing you can do, baby. Let the Lord, our God, guide you to the right answer. You have to be careful, though, because Satan will do everything in his power to show you the wrong way."

Solomon agreed as he hung on her every word and contemplated each of her examples. He didn't want to remain quiet, but he had to weigh each option. He was about to speak when a cold chill went up his spine. It captured his attention. He gasped.

"Solomon," his mother said, as his cold chill enveloped his body. "There is another option, too. It's one that we very seldom consider, since we are too preoccupied with the choices given to us."

"Give me an example."

"If I'm cooking you supper and offer you either Red Stripe Beef Stew or Ackee and Salt-fish, you're going to choose between those two dishes. It will never cross your mind that you have more than just those two choices. What if you don't feel like either of them is the right choice? Do you eat one or the other just to please your mama? Think about it, my child."

Her words sunk into him, as if God Himself had spoken to him through his mother. She was more than right. That was his answer. He did not have to take either side. There had to be another option.

"Are you still there son?"

"Yes Mama," he finally said with humility in his voice. "You are truly a godsend. You hit the nail on the head. That's exactly what I needed to hear."

"I know," she replied without hesitation. "That's what mamas are for. You got the best one."

He couldn't help but laugh. "Ha ha! You're absolutely right, Mama. You are the best. Thank you! Thank you for your words of wisdom and thank you for being my mama!"

She laughed. "That sounds so good."

"You are truly the best!"

"Are you going to call me more regular from now on?" she almost demanded.

"Yes, Mama," Solomon replied humbly. "I will call you every day and sometimes twice in one day."

"Good. Now you let God guide you as you take on this big decision of yours. I want to hear all about it when you finally get it resolved."

"Okay! You got it, Mama."

"I love you, baby."

"I love you, too, Mama. I have some things to think about. I'll talk to you tomorrow."

△△△

Just as Sanderson had said, for the past seven days, the Harvest Moon made its appearance on a nightly basis. Solomon thought and prayed about what his next course of action would be. Then it hit him. Whenever the Harvest Moon appeared, he would make sure to be present in the *Project Interstellar* building. He could then check out the other floors and the basement to see if anything was being generated from the facility to create the illusion of the extended Harvest Moon.

Ingram was the last one to leave and he made sure Solomon was alright before he left. "Do you need anything, Solomon? Can I leave a message with the guard?"

"Oh, no. I'm fine," Solomon responded nervously. In fact, he had been somewhat nervous all week, which did not go unnoticed by his boss. "Tell me, sir. Do you find the full moons showing up daily to be strange?"

"Does that bother you?"

"It is just strange. I want to look into it." He dropped his head. "I thought I could talk to you about it."

"Well, you have my private cell number, if you need to contact me for anything." He then approached his newest employee and got right in his face. "You've been noticeably impatient," he said. "I know something is bothering you, Solomon. I completely understand if it's personal, but I still need to know that you will handle it and it won't interrupt your progress here. I do believe I've gone over the open door policy. Did I not?"

"No. I mean, yes," Solomon responded while standing and facing Ingram. He didn't want to lie, but he couldn't tell the truth either. "It's my mother. I am sorry, but I always worry about my mama. She's not sick or anything. She's just getting to that age. You know?"

Ingram's features softened. "I understand, my friend. We have all kinds of programs and services to assist family members as well as employees. I'm not insinuating that your mother needs help, but it's always good to weigh your options, if you know what I mean."

"I know exactly what you mean," Solomon replied, trying to give the impression that he was breathing a sigh of relief.

Ingram glared while smiling. "Alright then. I'll leave you to your tasks and we'll talk again in the morning. The next time you talk to your mother, please give her my warmest regards. Won't you?"

Solomon nodded. "I sure will, Jeremy. I sure will."

"And don't worry about the Harvest Moon right now."

△△△

Solomon sat in his office with the lights out, waiting for everyone on the bottom floor to leave for the day. There was no one left on his floor, so there would be no questions about why he turned out the lights.

He asked the ground floor guard to notify him when it was just the two of them in the building, without trying to sound cloak and dagger. The guard agreed.

Solomon looked out his window, just after he placed his phone on mute. He then waited about 30 minutes after the last employee left. He just wished that Sanderson would have given him more information about where to look for evidence, since the project was a front for something far more sinister. She gave him no information to work with.

He found out that Sanderson had better security clearance than he did, yet she needed him to do her dirty work. She had explained to him that she needed him for other reasons as well. When at work, she had to stay extremely close to Ingram, and that meant she couldn't snoop around without him knowing. Also, Solomon was the new guy and a hero and wouldn't be questioned if he was someplace he shouldn't be. He wondered just how far he could push that, without losing the trust of his employer.

He put a couple of pairs of latex gloves in his jacket pocket, and made sure they didn't look too bulky. He felt anxious as he exited his office with a small flashlight in his hand.

He glanced around the hallways and saw no one. Slowly, he made his way to the elevator, avoiding places where all of the cameras were placed. At least the ones he knew about. He was being as careful as he could.

He stepped into the elevator and pressed an unfamiliar button. The one for the third floor. He had never been on that floor before. He had actually never been on any floors other than the ground floor and the top one.

When he thought about it, he was never given a grand tour like most employers gave.

He braced himself for anything out of the ordinary on the third floor. When the elevator doors opened, all that was revealed to him was a floor filled with cubicles. In fact, he couldn't see past the first several. There was a path to the left and one to the right, which passed a water fountain and the restrooms.

It would have been dark if it wasn't for the security lights every ten feet. There was still an ominous feel to the floor. He felt that it was because he was looking for something that he probably shouldn't find. His heart began to pound.

After a thorough walk-through, he realized that there wasn't anything other than a lot of cubicles, a meeting room, and a couple of manager's offices.

He walked casually so that he could tell Ingram he just wanted to see the rest of the building. That should cover him in case he ended up somewhere he was not supposed to be.

$$\triangle\triangle\triangle$$

He had the same luck with the other floors. After reaching the ground floor, he knew that all of the heavy machinery must have been in the basement.

Carl, the guard, motioned to him to go over to him. He had a smile on his face. Carl was in his mid to late 30s and it was evident he worked out. He had an impressive V-shape, even noticeable through his uniform, which was one size too big for him.

He had thick, black, curly hair and a thick mustache that placed him more in the 70s than current times.

Carl just finished a bite of his sandwich when Solomon walked up.

"Hey, Solomon. What cha' up to?"

Solomon tried to use his being nervous to his advantage. "It's still a little intimidating in this huge complex at night. I was just taking a break from work to take a look around."

"Especially after everything you've been through lately. Huh?" Carl wrapped up the rest of his sandwich so he could talk to Solomon. "Like I said before, if you need anything, just let me know. I know this building like the back of my hand." He playfully looked at the front of his hand and put on a faux fearful expression. He turned his hand over and sighed. He then laughed at his own joke. "Shoot," Carl said, unwrapping his sandwich, and taking a big bite. He chewed quickly so that he could answer Solomon's query.

Solomon tried to ignore the slurping and munching sounds. "For a project having to do with observing space, I have yet to find one telescope. I would assume Jeremy would have some on the roof."

Carl nodded and held up a finger so that he could finish his bite. "Yeah," he said, after taking a big gulp of coffee to wash down the food. "I was wondering when you were going to ask about that. I just figured that you and Jeremy hashed out all of that stuff when he hired you. You'd be surprised how many people don't like to ask questions when they get hired. Anyhow, we are linked somehow to the *Theodore Jacobson Observatory* on the campus of the University of Washington. Don't ask me how all of that technical stuff works, but it does. I think all of their data gets transmitted to us. Our scientists go there all the time. It's pretty cool. I've been there a couple of times now."

Solomon smiled. "That makes sense. Jeremy was recruited from the University of Washington. That worked out really well for the project."

"Oh, heck yeah!" Carl exclaimed. "I know there's more to it than that, but anything else, Jeremy will have to tell you himself. I'm just a working stiff. Ha ha!"

Solomon nodded and tried to laugh, but didn't want it to sound as fake as it would be. "I loved everything I have seen so far, Carl, but I would like to see the basement."

Carl's laughter halted as abruptly as it started. "Whoa, Solomon! The basement? Wow. Do you even know what you're asking me, man? I mean, seriously?"

Suddenly, there was complete silence. Solomon had a blank expression on his face. Carl just glared at him.

A smile slowly crept over Carl's face, and he started to chuckle. He then went into a full blown laugh. "Man! I'm just yanking your chain! Ha ha! You should have seen your face, Solomon! Of course, I can show you the basement! I mean, I do have the keys and everything! Ha ha! I have to do my rounds anyway, so you can come with me, okay?"

"Sure," Solomon replied, with a sigh of relief. "I would be happy to accompany you on your rounds, Carl. Can we start at the basement by any chance?"

△△△

Solomon was extremely disappointed when Carl told him that he usually started on the roof and worked his way down. He didn't want to do anything to prevent the guard from showing him the basement, so he agreed. He just wished that he would have talked with Carl first, before checking out the other levels.

Carl was very thorough with his walk-through. It was almost 2 A.M. when they made it back to the ground level.

Carl put his flashlight through his belt loop and rubbed his hands together furiously. "Are you ready for the basement? Ha ha!"

Solomon smiled weakly because he knew that he had to play Carl's game. "I don't know, Carl. It sounds sinister. I'm glad you're going to be there to guide me through it."

Carl nodded slowly, as he walked toward one of the elevators. "I hope you're ready for this."

He pulled out what appeared to be a credit card and slipped it into a slot that was practically invisible to the naked eye.

The wall by the elevator opened up to reveal a staircase going down. It was a spiral staircase made of rock with an iron railing.

Solomon could just look on in shock, as Carl pulled out his flashlight, turned it on, and slowly descended the stairs.

"Are you kidding?" was all Solomon could say as he reluctantly followed the guard downward.

CHAPTER TEN

Solomon was halfway down the staircase when he heard the door finally start to close. He then heard a loud crack and looked up to see what happened. The door was stuck open. It had only closed partially.

"Carl!" Solomon shouted before thinking it through.

Carl ran back up to where Solomon was and peered at the open door. "Not good," he whispered. "Not good, at all, Solomon."

He pulled out his Glock and slipped past Solomon, who was frozen on the stairs. He didn't want to expect the worst, but obviously, Carl thought it meant trouble that the door didn't close. Solomon looked around to see if there was anything he could use as a weapon.

He saw Carl sneak up to the door and look around. All of a sudden, he heard low grunts and the sound of a scuffle. He saw a figure dressed in all black struggling with the guard.

"Solomon!" Carl said. "Go down and find a phone or... use your cell!"

Solomon hurried down the rest of the stairs, as he heard footsteps coming down behind him. He glanced up and saw that Carl was still fighting off his attacker, which meant that there were at least two intruders.

Solomon nervously pulled out his phone but dropped it when he tried to take two stairs at a time. It clanked and bounced all the way down to the basement floor.

His heart raced, as he said a silent prayer and tried to retrieve his phone. He didn't even bother to look at his surroundings, but he thought he was going to be killed.

As soon as he reached the floor, he saw his phone and made a dash for it. As soon as he reached it, he felt a hard push from behind, which caused him to fall forward a few feet past his phone.

When he looked up, he saw a figure dressed in black with a ski mask and a small backpack. He knew right away that it wasn't Eric because the body shape and height were all wrong.

He jumped for the phone without any regard for his safety. The intruder had a 3 to 4-foot-long wooden stick that he used to hit Solomon's hands, every time he grabbed at his phone.

Frustrated, Solomon got to his feet and ran toward the middle of the room which was better lit, stopping short when he realized where he was.

The basement was huge. It was at least 200 square yards, with every inch filled with wonders.

To his left, he saw an extensive research lab secured within its own structure. The name, *Project Lab*, was embossed on a solid metal door with a keypad locking mechanism protecting it.

There were several desks in front of him with computers and various parts which looked to him to be replacement parts for telescopes, microscopes, and the computers themselves. For the most part, the desks were rather messy. On the walls in no particular order, were dozens of charts and graphs featuring the solar system, star formations, various constellations, individual planets, and of course, information on the Harvest Moon and the phases of the moon.

His mouth dropped open as he stood surrounded with information that he not only helped to gather, but that he wanted to see for himself. He was so caught up in the moment that he forgot about the intruder behind him. Then he felt something hard hit the back of his head and everything went black.

△△△

Once Solomon regained consciousness, he realized that he

was lying on the ground and was bound with duct tape wrapped around his hands behind his back. His feet were taped together as well. He saw Carl bound just as he was, lying on the ground next to him. Yet, it appeared that they were still in the basement. They were both at the bottom of the stairs. Carl was gagged, while he was not.

Two figures dressed in black stood before him. One had Carl's card that allowed him entrance to the basement. It didn't take Solomon long to figure out who one of them was.

"Andrea," he said, quietly and with disappointment. "Is that you?"

She took off her ski mask. It was Sanderson. "I couldn't tell you everything, Solomon."

"Why are you doing this?"

"I needed to know if you were really on my side. So we checked to make sure there are no cameras down here. It's strange how the most important floor of the project is without internal security."

"Maybe it was to lull the saboteurs into a false sense of security."

The voice was male and very familiar. Solomon looked around and saw Ingram standing near the wall of the lab with three armed guards, who were pointing their weapons at Sanderson and her accomplice.

"Sanderson, this is something no one expected."

She started to laugh. "Ha ha! Good one, Jeremy! You don't think I was smart enough to figure this one out? Is it because I'm a woman? Is that why you underestimated me?"

Ingram glanced at Solomon, then glared at Sanderson. "I never underestimated you, Andrea. I gave you the rope. What you decided to do with it was entirely up to you. It looks like you decided to hang yourself. It really is a shame, because you had so much potential. The only person who held you back for gender issues was you. It never mattered to me whether you were a man or a woman, but you were so gender-biased that you couldn't see past your own nose."

"You always thought you were smarter than me, Jeremy." She returned her comment with anger.

He raised a brow. "It was never about who was smarter. I would like to think that I am beyond playground tactics. I'm sorry if I ever gave you the impression that I thought myself smarter than those around me. I am simply part of a whole. A well-oiled machine, if you will. I figured that your pettiness and bitter disposition would eventually be your downfall. I knew that when I started working with you. I thought that I could overlook your personality flaws to see the bigger picture of who you are. You do have talent, my dear."

She looked like she didn't know what to say, and tightened her lips.

Solomon looked at both of them, then decided to say something. "Excuse me? Look. I am new at all of this and frankly, I am a little upset. The thought that I was brought into the middle of all this insanity upsets me. Since I have been brought into it, there is no reason why we can't all sit down like civilized adults and…"

"No one asked for your opinion, Solomon," Ingram responded, while still glaring at Sanderson. "I still don't know where you stand. You are my new employee and I practically gave you free run of the project, yet you sneaked down here. You are hard to figure out."

Solomon shook his head. "I don't know why. What you see is what you get. This is who I am. I'm not out to get anyone and I certainly don't plan on sabotaging anything that I don't know about."

Sanderson gave Solomon an angry look. "I thought you understood! You gave me the impression that you understood! Great! You've been a spy for Jeremy this whole time! Is that it?"

"No! I resent that."

She raised her voice. "I bet you told him about me and Eric taking you back to my place and discussing a plan to take down the project! You told him everything! Didn't you?"

"No!" Solomon hollered back. He didn't like to yell, but he felt he was pushed. "I didn't tell anyone anything! You just told him yourself, genius." Solomon rolled his eyes, "If you two want to fight, you should do it in the open! This whole spy thing makes my heart race and I don't like that one bit."

Ingram nodded to one of the guards and he went over to the other figure and carefully took the mask off. It was another female. This one was blonde and looked to be of high school age. The girl looked scared and confused, as she inched her way toward Andrea.

Sanderson placed her hands on the girl's shoulders and pulled her close.

Solomon and Ingram were shocked. They both knew a mothering instinct when they saw one.

"You've got to be kidding me!" huffed Ingram. "That's your... daughter?"

CHAPTER ELEVEN

T here was a moment of silence and then Ingram spoke again. "The resemblance is uncanny! You never told me you had any children, Andrea! As close as you and I had worked together and I never knew?"

"That's right," Sanderson replied in a soft voice. "I never told anyone about her. My mother has had custody of her. I just recently brought her back where she belongs—with me."

Solomon could not just watch in confusion the conversation going on between his employer and the woman who wanted to destroy his project. "Excuse me. All of this is very fascinating, but I have two requests. If you could untie Carl and me, I'm sure we could all sit down and discuss this like reasonable adults. Also, I would like to address quite possibly the more immediate concern of the present Harvest Moon. Please?"

Ingram and Sanderson stared at Solomon for a brief moment, then looked at each other.

Ingram sighed. "I am more than willing to put down my arms so that we may talk and lay everything on the table. My only request, besides not killing anyone, would be that there are no more lies. Frankly, I'm sick of all the lying."

Sanderson nodded at her daughter and the young girl went to untie Solomon and Carl. Once they were both free, Ingram instructed his men to lower their weapons, but to monitor what was going on.

Solomon helped Carl up and they both kept their distance from both Sanderson and Ingram. He said, "From what I can tell, you both care about each other a lot. You fight like a married couple."

"How could you betray me, Andrea?" Ingram asked, in almost a pleading tone.

"Betray you?" she shot back. "You're the one with this secret project! Do you think it's just coincidence that the project was up and running around the same time that the Harvest Moons began to appear in the sky?"

"You can't be serious!" was Ingram's only reply. Solomon noticed that the veins on his neck stood out as his face turned red. It was the first time he saw his employer so angry.

"What happened to our friendship?"

"Nothing has changed."

Ingram closed his eyes, mumbled something, then opened his eyes and looked at Sanderson. "I did everything to show you my trust and loyalty. You had access to everything concerning the project."

"Except this basement floor," she said with disdain. "I tried my best to get close to you, so I would have access to everything! You kept me from the most important part!"

Solomon looked at Ingram. He appeared to be hit with a cruel realization that she had not been honest. "Your words, just now. You basically came out and said that your goal from the beginning was solely to access my research. I…" He lowered his head sadly. "Is that true?"

"Uh… I'm going to look around and make sure nothing's broken," Carl said nervously, as he quickly made his way down past the desks.

Sanderson fell to her knees and wept. Her daughter came up and tried to comfort her. "Jeremy." Her voice cracked with emotion. "Jennifer here… is… your daughter."

Ingram turned pale as he narrowed his eyes at the girl. "No. How?"

"I was a fan of yours a long time ago, Jeremy. Your research and your whole attitude just sucked me into your world. We met at a faculty party. It was one that I did everything in my power to get invited to just to meet you. We drank, we partied. We spent one night together and the rest is history. When you didn't want anything else to do with me, I became despondent and tried to find a way to discredit you. Then this project came up and I joined you. Finally, I figured I could best get your attention by destroying you from within."

"Wait just one minute!" Ingram huffed. "None of that makes any sense! I remember having a drink with you, but that is all."

"Think a little harder."

"I never had any relations with anyone at those parties! I think you may have me confused with Professor Steiner. He played on the side of promiscuity. I'm afraid that all of this was for nothing. Since you have now blatantly admitted much more than I had anticipated, I'm afraid that I will have to call the authorities and…" He stopped short, lowering his tone. "I am trying to help humanity enjoy life. I'll have you know that I brought Solomon into the fold, because he has extensive knowledge of the Harvest Moon. I don't have a clue as to why there are so many Harvest Moons being observed on a continuous basis. It would have all been resolved by now. Solomon would have finished his research, had you not been constantly interrupting us with your break-ins and shenanigans."

It was Sanderson's turn to be confused. "I don't get it. I mean, what you're saying actually makes sense. It can't be true!"

"It is."

The voice came from the stairwell. It was very recognizable to Solomon.

"E-Eric?" Solomon stuttered while wondering if anything else would happen to classify the events as a legitimate soap opera. "Is that you?"

"Yes, sir," Eric replied while walking in from the staircase off to the side. "I know this is really confusing, but I might be able to shed some light on… well, everything."

Sanderson ran her hands through her hair and tugged at the roots. "Wait just a darn minute here! You were babbling like an idiot after we ran you through that dream machine!"

Solomon felt rage rise up inside him. "You did what to my friend?"

"I told you we have the dream machine." Andrea glared at Solomon.

"You knew it almost killed him before. Why would you take that chance again."

"I submitted to it, Solomon." Eric glanced around at everyone and seemed very much in control of his faculties. "I know. For a while, I was pretty much out there." He rushed to Solomon and gave him a big hug. "Let's not fight with them. I missed you, man!"

"I missed you too, my friend," Solomon replied, as he patted his back firmly. "It's nice to have you back."

"It's nice to be back," Eric said, as his expression became sober. "Now, back to the matter at hand. What no one, including me, realized, was that my dreams were becoming clearer each time Sybil's machine was used on me. Finally, everything was spelled out beautifully. I now finally understand what it was all about. My dreams are messages from my creator. God Himself has guided my journey from the very first dream. I don't know why I was chosen, but I am glad I was. So if you'll all please listen until I'm done, I'll tell you what's going on."

CHAPTER TWELVE

E ric had the floor.

"Alright, guys." Eric looked apprehensive but spoke clearly. "Whether you believe what I'm about to say or not, doesn't matter. But please listen. I have a feeling that it will all make sense soon."

As Eric stood in front of all of them, he looked pensive. "Look. I've never done anything like this before, but it has to be done. In the name of Almighty God!" He looked at everyone's expression quickly, as if he expected a certain reaction from one or more of the people present.

He nodded. "Now that my dreams have become crystal clear, I feel it is my duty to let everyone know," Eric nodded to the professor. "Professor Ingram. Even though I've seen it on the way here, can you confirm that the Harvest Moon has made yet another appearance in the sky?"

Ingram chuckled. "Of course, I can. I saw it on my way to the project. Is that what this is all about?"

Eric nodded. "In a matter of speaking. Yes. I know that Andrea thought that you had something to do with it. She thought that you wanted to push the end of the world by feeding on people's paranoia. She thought you faked a Harvest Moon. I can tell you right now that it's not fake. I mean, how can you fake something that everyone in the world can see? That's not possible. If we would have paid more attention, like my friend Solomon here, we would know that all we had to do was study the sky. There is so much to learn just looking through a telescope."

At the mention of his name, Solomon said, "True." He was concerned that he might have missed something in his own research and was eager to hear Eric out.

Eric continued, "When I was a kid, my sister, Sybil, and I used to love magicians. We thought that their tricks were real magic. We learned later on, like everybody does, that they are just tricks. The big thing for them is to show you what they want to show you while distracting you from the real trick. Satan's the same way."

"Is this going to turn out to be a talk about religion?" Sanderson said while grimacing.

"No, it is just a fact," Eric said. "You can't have a talk about people without mentioning the Creator or His enemy. They are both real whether we believe or not. I would suggest that those who don't should start paying more attention to events in the atmosphere. Because God is in charge of the universe and leaves messages there for people."

"Get to the point, son," Ingram gently urged.

"I am, Professor," Eric said while starting to pace. "Please, just let me finish."

Ingram nodded. "Okay."

Eric kept pacing with his hands behind his back. "Thank you. As I was saying, evil experts use tricks like a magician does. They have been distracting all of us. They used magic on you, Professor Ingram, to deflect you and keep you from concentrating on your research. They are behind the people who are trying to sabotage your project. You've been too preoccupied with work to notice. You believed Andrea was on the same page as you because she helped with the research. If so, the answers would have been right in front of her face. But she was looking for something different. Plus, Solomon never got to research anything. Instead, he got caught in the middle of you two, Professor, and Andrea. I'm sure there isn't much he has accomplished when it comes to his job, since he was hired just a short time ago. Even though he is a brilliant man."

"We know that," said Sanderson.

"But you were distracted."

"I wouldn't call it a distraction," Sanderson said defiantly.

"Brilliant minds are the easiest to distract," Eric said profoundly. "I looked that up. Einstein was always distracted by something or other. Solomon, Andrea, and Professor Ingram are the smartest people I have ever known. After my sister, of course. Yet it was simple for dark forces to keep you all preoccupied while they were at work destroying the world around us."

"We're not as smart as we think." Solomon had a spark of realization. "We interfered with God's plans last time when we announced the end of days. We messed with something we should not have. We need a clear path to the knowledge of God's will from now on."

"In a way what you say is true," Eric said, showing he was nervous again. "The evil one tricked us."

He studied everyone's reaction. Solomon gave him a knowing look. Eric smiled.

"Okay. As you have probably heard, I have had prophetic dreams from time to time," he said. "I was attached to a dream machine so others could know them. The thing is, there was someone who was trying to keep me from telling anyone what was really going on in the universe. It's like that thing I've heard people say about Satan being there when Christ was crucified. Satan did not know what was going to happen next. If he'd known Jesus was going to rise from the dead, he would have tried to stop the crucifixion. It could happen again when God's plan is fulfilled."

"I agree." Solomon stood up and clasped Eric's shoulder. "Satan is still alive and trying to mess with our thoughts."

"I would like to share my last dream."

"Please do." Everyone agreed.

"Here we go: *I was dreaming about the dream machine and my sister. I was given a series of electrical shocks. There were sounds of pops and crackles, and then the dream machine sputtered and fizzled out. Sparks flew all over the laboratory. Then I saw two witnesses to the electronic breakdown duck for cover until all was clear.*

"'Did we get that? Tell me we got that!' shouted the 54-year-old researcher.

"'We got it! We got it!'" said his female partner. 'We may have gotten it at the expense of my brother, but we got it!'" His voice cracked. "The voice was my sister, Sybil."

"The man stood up and looked at her. 'I know you love Eric, Sybil, but we needed to keep the machine attached to him until we had a dream that made sense to us. Ever since he became comatose we've been getting clearer dreams from him. We've recorded everything!'

"My sister, Sybil Tania, stood center stage in my dream. A tear rolled down her cheek, as she looked at me, her unconscious brother lying perfectly still on the table, wired into the machine. 'I still don't get it. He seems to have been fused with the machine. There's no way we can turn it off without killing him, Seymour.'

"'We have 42 variations of the same dream!' Seymour shouted, victoriously. 'All we have to do is piece each one together and we can predict the future."

"I felt her lean over my body and place her hands on my head. She said, 'I'm so sorry, Eric. I know that the machine did this to you, but once I found out, I couldn't pull you out. Please don't have any dreams where I die. I've been writing down all the names of the people in your dreams and I'm going to look for them. Isabella and Solomon Dancer are the two most prominent ones so far. If your dreams are real, then we'll need all the help we can get to set as many people free as possible—with the knowledge that Jesus is the way, the truth, and the life. I want you to know that as many times as you've been saved in your dreams, it made me get more interested in reading the Bible. I'm saved now, Eric, but I still don't like what we had to put you through. Seymour is saved too. I'll always remember what you told me before you went under for the last time. You said, "Always remember, sis, if you really want to know what's going on with God, watch for the signs of the times. There's a lot to be learned from the stars and the planets." You are helping us, Eric. Goodnight for now, my brother.'

"I watched as Seymour finished hooking up the recorded dreams to a link. Even though the machine had fizzled out, the message went out over the waves. I had left my body and was on the sidelines all the *time as I watched Dr. Seymour Caladasian and Sybil Tania operate the monitor."* Eric looked up. *"I watched a broadcast of my most current dream."* Then I woke up."

"What happened next?" asked Solomon. "Did people heed the warning?"

"Not many. The next thing I saw was the world in the first stages of the Apocalypse. My dreams were on television for awhile. Those who believed the message were saved. But many of them were killed for their faith."

"I remember what Sybil said in the dream. *'I know it is a matter of time before I am found. I'll do everything I can to send the message of the prophetic dreams out into the world. I hope my sacrifice will not be in vain.'* In the middle of the dream, I watched her walk away from the broadcast with tearful eyes. She opened the front door and looked at the night sky. She whispered my name and said that she knew I was responsible for representing God to a Godless world. I could tell that she thought I was dead. Yet her heart was filled with hope that she would see me again."

Eric looked around the room and smiled. "That is all I remember, because then my eyes popped open, and I sat up wide awake, my heart beating rapidly. My spirit was back in my body."

"It was a God thing." Solomon smiled. "Remember, God is in control."

"I'm sorry, Eric," Ingram said. "This is rather hard for me to swallow. I know that ties in with what Solomon and you worked on last year, but seriously. Is that all true?"

"It was my dream."

At that point Carl came running out from the back of the room. He was out of breath. "Guys. I tried to go out the back door and... wow." Sirens were blaring in the distance, even as he spoke.

"What is the matter?" asked Sanderson.

"I wouldn't leave the building if I was you."

"What is it?" yelled Sanderson. "What's going on? Tell us."

Tears started to roll down Carl's cheeks. "The sky! It's... all... copper colored."

"Maybe the rapture is coming." Solomon ran toward a window.

"No!" Jennifer jumped out, enraged. She glared at Eric. "It's not supposed to be now! Not now!"

"What do you mean? We aren't in control of the sky." Eric glared right back. "Even the angels in Heaven don't know when this age is going to end. How would you?"

Sanderson and Ingram were frozen in a state of shock, as they stared at Jennifer.

"Jennifer? Will you please explain?" Sanderson asked, with a timid voice. She looked blank as if she were in shock.

Jennifer turned toward her mother with a knowing smile. "Mother. You being an atheist, gave me all the leeway in the world to take a different route as your daughter." Her voice was soft. Andrea Sanderson looked on in disbelief and said nothing.

Professor Ingram stood nervously. "Now see here, young lad...!"

Eric stepped to her side. "Let her speak her peace."

Jennifer spoke firmly. "Bringing Solomon Dancer into the middle of our family problems was a stroke of genius, if I do say so myself. It was all so perfect."

"Who are you?" Carl blurted. "How do you know so much?"

She glanced at him with a flirtatious smile. "Ask my parents who I am. I am here to help everyone. Unfortunately,we are getting close to the end of the age."

"What do you suggest we do?" Carl's voice trembled.

"Repent." She smiled at him. Then all of a sudden, tears flowed. The smile was still there but faded slowly. A pained look swept across her face, as she dropped to her knees and wept openly.

Eric squatted down beside her, putting his arm around her. "It's all right."

Solomon stood beside him. "Is she crying for what I think?" he whispered.

"Yes," Eric replied.

"Without Jesus, I am nothing." She smiled through her tears.

Sanderson and Ingram rushed to Jennifer. Sanderson put her arms around the girl. Jennifer peered over her shoulder at Eric and

Solomon, smiling.

"I'm sorry, Jennifer," Sanderson groaned. "I should have been more of a mother to you. I am so sorry that I treated you like a sidekick. You deserve better."

"No, Mom," Jennifer replied, in her demure female voice. "You did the best you could. You did the right thing. Grandma was a good mother."

"Is there anything I can do," Ingram added. "It's obvious the girl has gone through a tremendous amount of stress. Perhaps, I could suggest some wonderful therapists."

Jennifer embraced Ingram. "Thank you, Daddy. I know I've been through a lot of pain during my life. All I need now is for someone to believe me and encourage me. I need my parents."

Carl was sitting on a box with his head in his hands. Solomon approached him and gently placed a hand on his shoulder. "Carl. Are you going to be okay? Eric and I have some experiences similar to what you might have seen outside. If you could describe it..."

Carl looked up in confusion. "Describe it? Seriously? It was like something out of my worst nightmare! There was an orange glow... everywhere! I mean, it was like looking through some kind of stained glass. There was also something else. You know when it's like really hot out and you see those wiggly heat lines? That! I saw that!"

"That may be a sign," said Eric.

Carl frowned. "Just a sign? What kind of a sign?"

"The rapture." Eric closed his eyes for a moment and then looked at Solomon. Their eyes locked.

Solomon looked at Eric with concern. "So is this it?"

"When Jesus comes for his children, He will come like a thief in the night," Eric replied. "If the two over there would have concentrated on the earth and sky, they would have seen the signs that you saw." He pointed to Sanderson and Ingram.

"It was really my fault!" Solomon said sadly. "If I would have done my job right, I could have seen this coming!"

"Then what?" Eric returned. "What would you have done, if

you'd known? Knowing and not knowing is the same thing. The only difference is that we were prepared the best we knew how. We believed the Bible. We're saved by the cross of Christ. It's not a last minute thing, Solomon. We knew that before. Now that we're faced with it, it's easy to say what we could have done or said, or who we could have been."

Solomon nodded. "You're right. It feels like a warning to me. I know you feel it too, Eric. My heart is breaking for everyone else who refuse to believe."

Solomon turned back to Carl. "Carl. What you saw is a real wake-up call. Jesus is coming back in all of His glory to claim those who follow Him. It's not too late for you to believe in Him. I know you're frightened, but Eric and I can help you. You need to make a decision. You can believe in Jesus."

"I don't understand." Carl had a look of panic on his face. He looked at Solomon, then at Eric. He burst into tears.

"You have the power of choice," said Solomon. "He doesn't want to be forced on anyone. We won't force you."

"Do you want someone to pray with you?" asked Eric.

"Yes of course. My mom's real religious." Carl laughed nervously. "Yes. I do believe."

"Oh my gracious." Solomon suddenly perked up and looked at Eric. "Eric! I need to call my mama!"

"Go ahead," Eric said, calmly. "If you want privacy, I'll pray with Carl."

Solomon rushed to a private corner by the research room and pulled out his phone. He dialed his mother's number as quickly as his fingers would allow him.

She picked up on the first ring.

Solomon's heart was heavy, knowing that he might not see his mother again. "I love you Mama."

"I know, baby," she replied. It was obvious that she was fighting back tears. "God put you where you are because that's where you need to be. I know that better than anybody. You're still my baby though and I miss you somethin' awful."

"I miss you too, Mama. A lot. The Apocalypse is soon, Mama.

Armies are gathering in the middle east. It is becoming a danger-ous world. I want you to come live with me."

"I would love to do that." Her voice broke. "We'll consider that as a possibility."

He couldn't contain his tears anymore. "This is bigger than you and me, Mama, and I know that God doesn't want to keep us apart. You've been my strength and my rock all these years. Your prayers have gotten me through some really bad times. Even when I didn't turn to God that much, you encouraged me."

"You were always a good boy. I didn't have to raise you too much, because you were always facing the right path without too much nudging. I don't know if I say it as much as I need to, but I am as proud of you as any mother could be of her son. Maybe more. I felt so loved when you were sitting in that hospital room, waiting for me to get back to my ornery self."

He laughed. "Yeah. I remember when you woke up out of your coma. You were hungry and nothing I got for you satisfied you. Ha ha!"

"Baby," she returned, as her tone became more serious. "I'm going to tell you again. You are on earth for a reason. So you need to do God's work."

"I know. I know. How could I forget, Mama? You drilled it into my head for as long as I could remember. I appreciate that, though. Because of you, I believe God is real. You can count on that!"

"That makes me happy." She paused. "You know what, Solo-mon."

"What is it, Mama?"

"When I was first alone with you as a mere baby, I would spend the summer nights outside on the porch with you in my arms. Rocking you back and forth as I lost myself in the night sky. There was healing in those stars and that sky. If I stared at it long enough, all the bad things of the day would be wiped away. All that was left in my heart was love. Love for you and for my God."

"I've always believed that, Mama."

"Good boy. I knew you'd remember."

"You know, I have studied the constellations for years now and found patterns within the stars that make me think of God and His creation. I remember when I first realized that. I felt this healing chill all over my body. I still feel that sometimes, like now talking to you."

"Bam!" Loud explosions and screams were suddenly audible from outside and in the basement.

"Mama. I have to go now."

"What is that noise, Son?"

Solomon felt fear. "I pray to my Father in heaven that we will see each other soon, Mama."

"Yes! I'll see you soon, baby. God willing."

After her last word, the phone went dead, followed by rapid beeps. He put his phone away in his pocket and slowly walked back to Eric and Carl.

He didn't see Jennifer, Sanderson, or Ingram anywhere.

"Where are the others?" Solomon asked, frantically.

Eric cleared his throat and looked like he was in some pain. "They're gone, Solomon. Apparently, Jennifer was very convincing. They all left together. I prayed with Carl while you were gone."

"Praise Jesus!" Carl called out, with conviction, and a wide smile. His eyes sparkled with rebirth. "I feel so clean inside."

Solomon gently slapped Carl's shoulder. "Great to have you aboard!"

"How's your mom?" Eric asked, with concern. "Is everything okay?"

"She is fine," Solomon returned. "I want to either go home or bring her out here."

Eric turned to Carl. "What about you, Carl? Are you okay?"

"Yeah. I'll just hang out with you guys."

"Do you have family that you are concerned about?"

Carl shook his head. "Naw. Not really. I'm an only child and I never talk to my cousins and people like that. My parents died some time ago in a plane crash. My dad was the pilot. Don't get me wrong, he was the best pilot ever! They just flew into a freak storm. They were notified of it, right as he flew into it. Everyone I've talked to since said there was nothing anyone could have done about it. My dad actually kept him and my mom in the air longer than anyone else would have. Small consolation, though. I'd rather have them here with me now."

Solomon felt like he needed to go someplace else. "Would you like to take a little trip now and get away from this mess?"

Eric grinned and looked at Solomon, then back at Carl, who looked wide-eyed and then laughed. "Yes. You guys are not going to believe this, but I have my pilot's license for small aircraft and I also just so happen to have the keys to the plane I was trained on. I know the instructor, personally. He'll let me borrow it. Let's take a little trip."

Solomon became excited momentarily. His excitement faded almost as quickly as it arrived. "Wait! How are we going to get to the airfield from here without transportation?"

"Well," Carl stated. "If my Dodge is still out in the parking lot then we should be good to go!"

"Let's do it!" Solomon exclaimed as the trio worked their way up the stairwell and outside.

Eric said, "Where can we go? Maybe the grand canyon or Colorado Rockies."

Solomon burst out, "Let's go see my mama."

"Okay, Mama's boy."

CHAPTER THIRTEEN

The three men were all in shock when they moved slowly toward the front door and walked into excruciating heat outside. There was a bronze haze over everything, just like Carl had said. Also, the air was shimmering, like Carl described. People were running up and down the street screaming in terror. Young men were looting, and there were obvious acts of violence in the street.

Solomon allowed his thoughts to take over. He thought of the little gadgets that people put on their front lawns at Christmas time, that flashed stars all over the front of their homes. That was how the golden moons had appeared night after night. It was Sanderson. She had done it. When he said something, Eric looked guilty. The project had failed.

"The world is completely out of control," said Solomon. He turned to his friends with a serious expression. "No matter what happens, we cannot get involved with what's going on here. We have to look past everything and run, first to the car and then to the plane."

Eric and Carl both reluctantly nodded. Carl nudged Eric and pointed to the back end of the parking lot where his Dodge Neon was parked. Solomon breathed a sigh of relief when it appeared the car was not damaged. "Okay, run," he said

Carl made a mad dash to his car. He fumbled for his keys in his pocket. When he found the right key and opened the door on the driver's side the other two arrived. Eric reached the car, opened the back door, and jumped in, closing it behind him. Solomon opened the passenger side front door and practically dove into the seat.

Solomon heard a noise and slowly turned around. Jennifer was running their way. "It's Jennifer," he called out. "Wait for her."

"Run," Eric called out to her, as he threw open the door and she jumped in.

Carl started the engine and hit the gas. "Make sure all of the windows are rolled up and the doors locked."

Solomon said, "Let's get out of here."

Suddenly, a monstrous blast rumbled through the area, the resulting vibrations were sent through the entire area and rattled the car like an earthquake. It was like moon sized balloons were popping all over the sky.

Skidding out of the parking lot, Carl did not hit the brakes for anything. The rumbling became fainter and the vibrations lighter as they got further away from the explosion.

Solomon started to breathe easier, until he saw that most of the road in front of them was missing. All that was there was a large smoldering pit with fire and fumes shooting upward. "Carl! Stop!" he yelled.

Carl slammed on the brakes and turned the steering wheel sharply. The car rolled over several times, then finally came to a rest at the edge of the pit. "What the heck?"

Eric looked at Solomon with total shock. "It's not supposed to end like this, Solomon. It's not supposed to end like this. I don't know how I know, I just do." His voice was trembling.

Solomon smelled leaking gas. Fearing what might be next, he yelled, "Jump. Everyone jump. Now!"

The soil on the pit crumbled beneath the weight of the vehicle and it moved. Yelling, Solomon jumped. He saw three people flying through the air before he heard the explosion. The last thing Solomon saw, before passing out, was a burst of flames.

The next thing he knew he was lying in a hospital, with Carl in the bed beside him. "Where are Eric and Jennifer?" he asked the nurse.

"Not sure who you mean. But the other injured were taken to a different hospital."

"Do you think we could go see them?"

"You are not well enough to do too much," the nurse said. "You still need rest."

Solomon looked at Carl. "We can go see my mama for a couple of weeks. Then maybe we'll be strong enough to find Eric and Jennifer."

"Good idea."

Epilogue

Solomon learned that the *Project Interstellar* was destroyed in the blast. A bomb had gone off inside where someone was creating the fake moons.

As for Colonel Andrea Sanderson, she was able to help Professor Jeremy Ingram remember the night of their rendezvous when Jennifer was conceived. This made working conditions a little easier for both of them.

When Solomon and Carl were well enough to travel, they bought plane tickets to Portland to recuperate at the home of Solomon's mother, Calista. Carl became a best friend, like a brother. He said that he was quite happy to finally have a family.

Once the friends had recuperated, they met again in Seattle. It was a warm June night. Stars were out. A cool breeze blew across the park. The Harvest Moon was full and bright. All was peaceful. Professor Jeremy Ingram called me today," said Solomon. "He says he has a job for me."

Eric threw his cap at Solomon. "Don't take it."

The End

To be continued in:

Shoot for the Stars

Summer Lee is the author of 28 novels. She worked as a newspaper reporter before turning her attention to writing books full time. She lived in Southern California where she's hard at work on her next novel. Summer Lee is the pseudonym for author, Verna Hargrove. Please visit her at www.SummerLeeAuthor.com.

Made in the USA
Coppell, TX
29 September 2021

63199872R00055